NA...

T.. CASE: *Investigate the sudden and suspicious death of Sarah Amberly, the wealthy woman who is Nancy's next-door neighbor at the Plaza Hotel.*

C.. CT: *Nancy's on her own, and no one will talk ...ner except Maximilian, the waiter who seems to know everything about everybody.*

SU..ECTS: *Jack Kale, Sarah Amberly's nephew. He's been given everything, so why does he steal?*

Alison Kale, Sarah's younger sister. Is she crazy or just jealous of her sister's wealth?

Pieter van Druten, Sarah's fiancé. He has lots of money of his own—why would he do away with the woman he loves?

Madame Rosa, Sarah's tarot card reader. Is she helping Sarah or frightening her to death?

COMPLICATIONS: *House detective Joe Ritter has caught Nancy in Sarah's suite. He thinks she could be guilty of robbery—and murder.*

Books in The Nancy Drew™ Series

No. 21 RECIPE FOR MURDER
No. 22 FATAL ATTRACTION
No. 23 SINISTER PARADISE
No. 24 TILL DEATH DO US PART
No. 25 RICH AND DANGEROUS
No. 26 PLAYING WITH FIRE

THE NANCY DREW FILES™ CASE·25

RICH AND DANGEROUS

Carolyn Keene

AN ARCHWAY PAPERBACK
Published by SIMON & SCHUSTER

New York   London   Toronto   Sydney   Tokyo   Singapore

This book is a work of fiction. Names, characters, places and incidents are either the product of the author's imagination or are used fictitiously. Any resemblance to actual events or locales or persons, living or dead, is entirely coincidental.

An Archway paperback
first published in Great Britain
by Simon & Schuster Ltd in 1992
A Paramount Communications Company

Copyright © 1988 by Simon & Schuster Inc.

Simon & Schuster Ltd
West Garden Place
Kendal Street
London W2 2AQ

NANCY DREW, AN ARCHWAY PAPERBACK
and colophon are registered trademarks of Simon & Schuster Inc.

THE NANCY DREW FILES is a trademark
of Simon & Schuster Inc.

Simon & Schuster of Australia Pty Ltd
Sydney

A CIP catalogue record for this book is
available from the British Library

ISBN 0-671-71641-7

Printed and bound in Great Britain by
HarperCollins *Manufacturing*

RICH AND DANGEROUS

Chapter

One

N<small>ANCY</small> D<small>REW</small>, PLEASE meet your party at the registration desk in the main lobby—"

The words filtered into eighteen-year-old Nancy Drew's mind from what seemed like miles away. At last, she really was at the Plaza Hotel, away from River Heights, away from her detective work, and all ready to meet her dad for a long weekend in New York City.

Nancy made her way to the registration desk, her bright blue eyes taking in everything. Bellhops in immaculate dark blue uniforms walked purposefully over the thick forest-green-and-rose-patterned carpeting, while the hotel's fashionably dressed clientele ambled through the lobby, past glittering shops and newspaper stands that offered periodicals from all over the world.

Good old Dad, thought Nancy with an appreciative smile. He certainly knows how to pick a hotel.

It was going to be great spending the weekend in New York. Of course, the real reason for the trip was that Carson Drew was attending the annual Interpol convention. His work at his law firm often involved him in matters that fell under the jurisdiction of the international police organization. But between meetings he was sure there'd be time for the two of them to go to the theater, museums, and fine restaurants. Nancy planned to do some shopping while her father was busy at the convention.

"Hi, Dad!" she called. Carson Drew was standing at the desk, waiting for her. With his handsome profile and his dark hair, slightly graying at the temples, he looked the part of a successful attorney.

"Hello, Nancy!" he called back, waving. "Ready to check in?"

"Yes," she said. "I was just wandering around, mesmerized by this place. It's so elegant."

"And this is only the lobby." Carson laughed. "Wait till you see where we're staying. It's one of the penthouse suites."

Nancy threw her father an amused look. "You mean the ones they reserve for royalty?"

"Well, the last person to stay in it was Prince Ururu of Rarotonga, I'm told. Apparently, he came to the States for his annual fishing expedition, but he had to leave early—some kind of trouble in paradise. He left his gear in one of the closets, but I told the manager we could work around it."

"Fantastic! How did you rate such a place?"

"I guess Interpol is showing their appreciation for my services," Carson answered modestly, handing Nancy the registration book.

"I'm impressed, Dad," Nancy said, signing in. "But not surprised. You're one of the hardest-working people I know."

A good-looking hotel clerk handed Nancy a key. "Thank you, Miss Drew," he said. "Have a pleasant stay."

"Thanks," Nancy replied as she slipped her arm into her father's.

"Of course, I never did tell you about Great-uncle Drew, the Archduke of Hapsburg," Carson joked, leading her to the elevator. "Maybe *that's* how we got the penthouse. . . ."

With a laugh, Nancy stepped onto the mahogany-paneled elevator and pressed *P*. This weekend was going to be everything she'd imagined it would be—she could just tell. She allowed herself a smile of pure happiness as the elevator whisked them upward.

3

At their floor, Carson stepped through the elevator doors. "Well, here we are. The building doesn't go any higher than this."

Nancy followed him out into the thick-carpeted hallway and down the long corridor. Soon he stopped at a set of intricately carved double oak doors and drew out his key.

"The suite you ordered, Miss Drew." Carson opened the door and switched on the light. They were inside a room the size of a small house, filled with antique furnishings. A leather divan was placed opposite an intricately carved marble fireplace, and two leather club chairs flanked it.

"This is my room—" Carson opened a door and showed Nancy a spacious room decorated in understated masculine tones. "And just across this little hall—" Now he flung open the door to Nancy's room. The first thing that caught her attention was the large window with the panoramic view of Fifth Avenue. Then her eyes took in the silk damask wall covering, decorated with work by artists Nancy had only seen in museums.

"I had the bellhop bring up your bags," said Carson with a satisfied smile. "You can unpack if you like. I've got to make a few phone calls before dinner."

"Oh. Well, Dad, knowing you, a few phone calls may take quite a while. If you don't mind, I think I'd like to wander around for a bit." With a wink and a smile, Nancy was out the door.

* * *

4

An hour later Nancy stepped off the elevator at the top floor and headed back to her suite. The hotel really was as magnificent as she'd always heard.

She was about to fish her key out of her bag when the door to the neighboring suite burst open, and a knot of four people poured out into the hallway, creating a commotion that made Nancy stop and listen.

The group was obviously dominated by an old lady—well, not old exactly; she was probably only in her fifties, but the obvious signs of ill health made her seem older. She was thin—emaciated really—and her pale face was made up with ruby-red lipstick and blusher, which matched the ruby earrings she was wearing. But the rich color couldn't hide her pallor.

Walking slowly on the arm of a handsome middle-aged man, she was complaining to her companions in a voice more powerful than Nancy would have thought possible.

"Why can't one of you keep track of these things?" she demanded. "My medicine is the only thing that's keeping me alive. Why is it that you allow it to run low so often? Sometimes I think you're all stealing it to sell on the black market!"

The three other people in the party looked at one another, as if to say, "You know how she is when she's in one of her moods." As they passed, Nancy pretended to have trouble with her key,

5

taking the moment to get a better look at her weekend neighbors.

There was a tall middle-aged woman with stringy hair, dressed in clothes at least ten years out of date. She cringed at the old woman's every word, as if she were being tortured rather than reprimanded. Nancy thought she detected a resemblance between the two women—at least, in their faces. Their attitudes, however, could not have been more different.

The man who was guiding the old woman was dressed in a conservative dark blue suit. He had a look of studied patience, as if he were merely waiting for the woman to blow off her steam. He was a distinguished-looking man and appeared to be totally at ease in the very expensive suit he was wearing.

The fourth member of the party was the most interesting to Nancy. For one thing, he was one of the handsomest guys she had ever laid eyes on. He looked about twenty-two, with jet black hair and light blue eyes—a killer combination. He was hanging back from the rest of the party, toying with the key in the lock.

"There," he said at last, jogging to catch up with the others as they rounded the corner of the hall on their way to the bank of elevators. Nancy could hear him speaking. "Here's your key back, Aunt Sarah. Though why we even bother to lock the place is beyond me."

"Goodness knows, you'd leave the door wide

open if it was up to you, Jack," his aunt Sarah huffed.

"After all, that's what hotel security's for, isn't it?"

"Yes, you'd leave everything to others, wouldn't you?" the old lady shot back. "If it were up to you, I'd run out of medicine completely!"

"Now, now, Aunt Sarah, you know it's your own fault. Lately you've been wolfing down that stuff. Remember, we have to send to Mexico for it."

They were gone now, in the elevator, out of earshot. Nancy shook her head in amusement. Rich people could be as strange as everyone else, she knew. Once again she put her key in the keyhole, this time for real.

That's when she noticed something strange. The door that the handsome young man had appeared to be locking was, in fact, not locked at all. Instead, it was about half an inch open.

That's odd, Nancy thought. He took so much time at the door; he must have left it open on purpose. But why?

She walked to the door, intending to close it. But as she moved forward, she stumbled and grabbed at the doorknob. The door swung wide open, pulling Nancy into one of the most opulent rooms she had ever seen. Crystal chandeliers, edged in gold, threw soft, shimmering light on the plush furniture. This single main room was the size of the entire Drew suite.

Somehow, as impressed as she had been by everything she'd seen at the Plaza, this was the most incredible part of all. Huge windows looked out on Central Park. The entire city lay beneath her, as if curled up at her feet. Nancy took the view in with a sigh, then reminded herself that she wasn't even supposed to be in there.

A huge oak table in the center of the room caught her eye. On it, several cards were laid out in a distinct pattern. Nancy recognized them as fortune-telling tarot cards.

She went over to take a closer look at them. Too bad she knew nothing about the tarot, she thought. The cards were extremely interesting looking. There was one of a hanged man, one of a sad boatman paddling across a river, several with swords on them, and even one that said Death, with a picture of the Grim Reaper on it.

Nancy shuddered involuntarily. It was all vaguely creepy.

Just as she was about to leave, Nancy caught a soft, rhythmic scratching noise coming from behind the closed door of one of the bedrooms. Her senses immediately alert, she stood still and strained to hear. Could there be a prowler in the suite?

There was the noise again! Making up her mind, Nancy strode over and flung open the door to the bedroom. If there was anyone there, she'd have the advantage of surprise.

She almost laughed out loud when she saw the pigeon on the ledge outside the window. It was scraping its claws along the granite. So that was her prowler! Boy, Drew, you really *do* need a vacation, she reproved herself.

Just then she heard the soft creak of the suite's front door, and instinctively she ducked inside the open bedroom and pulled the door closed.

Her heart pounding, Nancy watched through the keyhole as someone stepped into the suite's main room. It was the gorgeous guy. He looked around quickly to make sure he wasn't being observed. Then he smiled tensely and walked over to a desk in the corner, opened a drawer, and took out a wad of bills. As he fanned them, Nancy was almost positive she could see Benjamin Franklin's face on every one. They were hundred-dollar bills!

Looking over his shoulder again, the young man pocketed the money and went out quickly, this time locking the door for real.

Nancy let out a sigh of relief and leaned against the wall. No way could that have been his own money, she thought. He'd acted too sneaky. He had to be stealing from his own family, and with a smile, too!

For the first time since she'd ducked inside, Nancy looked around at the room she was in. It was an absolute shambles. Clothes were strewn all over the bed—women's clothes. By the looks

9

of them, Nancy could tell they belonged to the woman with the stringy hair. This must be her bedroom.

On the desk by the window were several pieces of crumpled paper. Nancy didn't touch them. Her sense of propriety told her she had already ventured much too far into these people's private world.

She turned to go, but stopped short to avoid stepping on a piece of paper on the floor. When she looked more closely at it, her blood turned to ice water, and she felt a cold chill travel up her spine. Scrawled all over the paper, in a spindly, maniacal hand, were the words "KILL . . . KILL . . . KILL!"

Chapter

Two

DISTURBED BY THE violent words she'd just read, Nancy hurried back to the suite she shared with her father. Something obviously wasn't right in the suite next door. That note was really weird, and so was the theft she'd just witnessed. What was going on?

As she came through the door she saw her father lying on a chaise, his hand curled around the telephone. He was saying, "I see. So you're going to need an injunction from the authorities here to break into their computer system. . . ."

His eyes brightened when he saw her. "Hi,

honey, I'm going to be a while," he whispered, covering the mouthpiece of the telephone for a moment. "The chief of police from the Netherlands is kind of thorough."

"It's okay," Nancy replied softly. "I want to do some more exploring, anyway."

It didn't matter what plans she'd had for this trip—she was just about to change them. Someone might be in danger; she had to help.

"KILL, KILL, KILL." What an awful message! Nancy couldn't shake the image of the scrawled note, and all the way to the elevator, the faces of the old lady and her three companions played across her mind. Why would anyone who looked as rich as the young man have to steal? And why had the timid woman written such a horrible, hostile message?

Nancy stepped into the elevator and pressed *L*. She could just imagine her best friends, Bess Marvin and George Fayne, shaking their heads in disapproval. They had made her absolutely promise not to get involved with any mysteries on this trip. Now here she was, tiptoeing around in strangers' suites and reading their notes.

The elevator opened and Nancy headed for the Palm Court, the elegant café set in the center of the lobby. It was like an island surrounded by hundreds of stately palms. The air was filled with the sounds of a string quartet. Maybe Bess and George were right. Maybe she had forgotten how to relax.

"One?" The blond maître d' approached Nancy with a smile.

"Yes, please," Nancy replied.

Taking her seat at a small marble table toward the back, then looking over the menu, Nancy let herself forget the people in the suite next door. The quartet's music washed over her, and suddenly she felt terrific. There were so many wonderful things to look forward to this weekend! The hotel was right on Fifth Avenue, across from Central Park. And in every direction there were terrific shops, where the finest designers in the world sold their wares. Of course, there was Tiffany's right on Fifth—always a fun place to do some heavy window-shopping.

Nancy made a mental note to call her boyfriend, Ned Nickerson, at Emerson College later that night. Ned loved the city as much as she did, and she wanted to tell him about her stay.

"A good for nothing, that's all you are!" The woman's dramatic voice boomed out, catching Nancy's attention. It came from behind her, on the other side of a thick row of potted palms. And there was no mistaking that voice, either. It belonged to the old woman she'd seen earlier— the one the gorgeous guy had called Aunt Sarah. Fate seemed to be throwing Nancy and her penthouse neighbors together.

Turning around, Nancy could see through the palm leaves that the elderly woman was addressing her remarks to her handsome young nephew.

"Yes, I think I have a perfect *right* to know where you go at night. I'm paying for it, am I not? Your uncle Joshua worked for every penny of the money you are tossing away! I'd like to make you work for that money and then see how careless you'd be with it!"

Nancy didn't hear the young man's reply, because just then the waiter came up and asked for her order.

"Good day, miss, my name is Maximilian—what may I get for you?"

Nancy looked up. Her waiter was a dark man, extremely short and bald, with a large walrus mustache. His accent was vaguely Eastern European.

The strange thing about him was that he didn't look at Nancy when he spoke. His eyes were riveted on the table on the other side of the palms. Obviously, he had heard every word of their argument.

"Oh! I haven't really decided," said Nancy, her eyes falling down to the glossy beige menu. "Just bring—let's see—any of the pastries. Something with chocolate—and some decaffeinated coffee, please."

"The éclair is exceptional today," he said, his eyes still on the other party.

"Fine. An éclair then."

"Don't think you can get to my soft spot this time!" The woman's voice filtered through the potted palm.

"Always the same, always the same . . ." the waiter muttered, transfixed.

"Excuse me?" Nancy asked.

Now the waiter caught Nancy's eye, and he shook his head slowly.

"Those people over there, they think their money makes up for their bad manners. Every day it's the same thing."

"Oh? They come here a lot?"

"They come here three or four times a year, miss, on vacation. They always stay in the same suite. I have waited on them for years." He looked Nancy up and down. "I see you are curious, miss. Yes?"

Had she been so obvious about her interest? "Well, perhaps a little," she replied casually. "I believe they're my neighbors."

"Well, I shall tell you, then," said Maximilian, with a little mock bow. "The woman is Sarah Amberly—perhaps you have heard of her? The wealthy widow from Boston. Since her husband passed away, she's worth more than many small countries. She's yelling at her nephew, Jack Kale. She scolds him, but she lets him steal from right under her nose."

So he *had* been stealing!

"She raised him, you know," the waiter continued. "And she spoiled him rotten. Now, she complains." With a derogatory snort, Maximilian made his contempt known.

"What about the others?" Nancy couldn't help

her curiosity, and the waiter seemed eager to supply her with any details she might want. "Who's the other woman?"

"Oh, yes, the poor thing—" With this, the waiter circled a finger by his temple. "It's Mrs. Amberly's younger sister, Alison Kale. Crazy, you know? She is very timid, but inside, so angry."

"Oh?"

"And the other man, with the graying hair, is Mr. Pieter van Druten—another delightful person. He's got millions from his diamond mines, but that's not enough for him. He's trying to get the old woman's money, too!"

"Really? How?"

"By marrying her, I suppose. Even now, he stays in her suite at her expense. She says this is a small repayment since he keeps her from loneliness, but I say the man is a sponge. Her dead husband was a good man—better than any of them. He was a man who worked for his money. These people are nothings, just idle rich who do nothing. They are dirt."

"Well, you certainly know a lot about them," Nancy observed. Maximilian's attitude was so bitter and angry that she felt sorry for the man.

"Know about them!" With that the waiter chuckled. "My dear miss, a servant sees many things, many things. I know much more than that, I assure you—for a small consideration, of course."

He's asking for a bribe! Nancy smiled and looked away. "I'm not a reporter, you know. I'm not in the business of buying information."

Smiling broadly now, the waiter turned to walk away. "If you should change your mind . . ."

But Nancy pretended not to hear. It was all intriguing, but she wasn't going to get any more involved than she already was. And there was no way that Nancy Drew would ever pay for information—not when she could get it herself, that is.

"Good night, Dad."

It had been a long, full day, and Nancy was tired. She and her dad hadn't had time to eat until after nine o'clock. Fortunately, dinner at the Oak Room, the Plaza's most exclusive restaurant, had been fabulous. And she and her father had finally gotten a chance to catch up.

The two of them had always been close because Carson had been both mother and father to her after Nancy's mother died. He had a housekeeper, though. Hannah Gruen was wonderful and like a mother to Nancy, but she couldn't replace her real one, of course. So Carson and Nancy had had to be a special team—good friends, real partners.

Lately, though, they hadn't had as much time for each other as they'd once had. Nancy was grown-up now, and Carson's successful career kept him busy. Yes, dinner together had been a precious time, but now he'd had to turn in early.

Smiling happily, Nancy picked up the phone beside her bed and dialed Ned Nickerson's number. He'd be back in his room at his fraternity house by now.

As she sat there listening to the ringing, Nancy continued to think about Sarah Amberly. There was something about her and her family—about Maximilian the waiter, too—something that drew her toward them, that *attracted* her. Was it Jack Kale's handsome face? Nancy didn't think so, but then . . .

"Hello?"

The voice coming through the receiver startled her out of her reverie. "Ned! Is that you?" Of course she knew it was; the warm rush that coursed through her when he answered told her it was.

"Nan! Hi!"

He sounded terrific. Nancy felt her heart lift. "Hi, Ned."

"Where are you calling from? The Big Apple?" he asked.

"You crazy old woman!" Nancy jumped about a foot off the bed when she heard the female voice shouting from the Amberly suite! "Don't you see you're being duped? He's not what he seems to be, I tell you! He's not what you think!"

"Nancy? Are you still there?" Ned's voice broke in, bringing Nancy back to herself.

"Uh, yes, Ned, I'm here," she stammered. "But there's some sort of argument going on next door, and I can't really hear you. Could I call you back in five minutes?"

"Sure, Nan. Talk to you then."

The phone clicked. Nancy hoped she hadn't offended Ned. In the past, there had been times when her detective work had put a strain on their relationship. They'd finally been able to sort all that out, though, and Nancy felt sure, down deep, that she could count on his support.

Sarah Amberly was shouting again, in that booming, intimidating voice of hers. "You're a fool, Alison! A complete and utter fool! And don't go telling me my own business. I don't have to put up with you, you know. I do it only out of the goodness of my poor, tired heart."

But Alison, who had seemed so fearful before, did not seem at all intimidated now. In fact, she seemed to be a different person altogether.

"You old loon! Don't you see he's dangerous? He leads you around by the nose. You'll be sorry, Sarah, mark my words! Sorry you were ever born!"

"I don't want to hear another word! Not another word!" Sarah Amberly was screaming now, and she definitely sounded shaken.

"Very well, then—you can throw your life away if you want. I tried, God knows! I tried—" And then there was silence.

The silence was soon interrupted by a low

moaning sound. And now the voice was saying something—something Nancy couldn't quite make out.

Rushing into the hall, Nancy caught sight of Alison Kale retreating down the corridor. It sounded as if she were muttering angrily to herself.

And now, standing outside the open door of the Amberly suite, Nancy could hear plainly—the unearthly moan was the voice of Sarah Amberly. And the word she was repeating over and over was by now a desperate cry—*"Help!"*

Chapter
Three

NANCY THREW OPEN the carved wooden door of the neighboring suite and rushed in. From the living room, she could see into Sarah Amberly's room. The woman was lying half on her bed and half on the floor. Her faded blond hair was undone—it spilled over her shoulders.

The moment she saw Nancy her eyes lit up. "My—my medicine—" she managed to say, twitching her fingers in the direction of a carved mahogany bureau across the room.

On the table Nancy spied a small ivory container. She shook out the contents into her hand—there were ten pale green tablets.

"One, just one, dear—any more would be dangerous . . ." Sarah moaned. Nancy put a tablet in the woman's fingers and rushed to the bathroom for water.

When Nancy came out, Sarah Amberly was already sitting up on the edge of the bed. She grabbed the water and eagerly drank it down.

"Thank goodness you came," she murmured, and leaned back against a pillow. For one long terrifying moment, her eyes closed. But when she opened them again, she seemed to be feeling much better. "Pardon my appearance, dear—"

"Oh, please," Nancy replied, holding up the ivory container. "Where should I put these?"

"I don't know who keeps moving them! Unless it's me, of course—my memory does fail me. Let's see, why don't you put them here, on my night table where I can reach them when I need one. They're the only things standing between me and eternity, dear, the only things."

With a smile, Sarah twisted up the ends of her pale hair and tucked a pin into it. "I knew you'd be coming, but I wasn't sure when."

Nancy's face must have shown her confusion, but Sarah just laughed. "If you don't believe me, go to the table in the living room and you'll see what I mean."

Sarah followed Nancy into the main room. There on the oak table were a number of tarot cards arranged in a circle. In the center was a single card, lying facedown. "Turn it over, dear. You'll see," said Sarah.

Nancy gently lifted the card and turned it over. On its face was a picture of three young girls dressed in what looked like clothes from the Middle Ages. They were smiling and dancing around a maypole.

"It is the Three of Cups, the card of friendship," Sarah explained. "You see, the cards never lie. My last reading indicated I would make a new friend—a young girl, someone pretty and lighthearted and good. And here you are!" The woman chuckled, obviously pleased with herself.

"Not only did you arrive as predicted," she continued with a laugh, "you also saved my life. My dear, I am terribly grateful. When my strength returns, I will certainly shake your hand. Come help me to the couch, and tell me your name."

"It's Nancy, ma'am. Nancy Drew," she said.

"Now, now, you must call me Sarah, since we're fated to be friends," said the fragile woman taking her seat. "Soon I'll be feeling fit. It won't be long. My medicine has remarkable powers."

The color was already returning to Sarah's face, replacing the ashen gray. And for the first time, she seemed to relax.

"What kind of tablets are they?" Nancy asked, unable to contain her curiosity.

"Oh, oxytomicin or some such name. It's made

23

from a flower grown in the mountains in Mexico. It's not yet approved by our government, but fortunately, I'm able to get it as part of a research project. I suppose with my condition they feel there's nothing to lose! So—I may look like a woman, but I'm really just a guinea pig."

Nancy felt herself relaxing as Sarah Amberly talked to her. Here in her own suite, Sarah wasn't the dominating personality she seemed to be when Nancy had first seen her.

"Now, sit down, Nancy. After a rescue like that, we both deserve a treat. I'll call room service. What will you have? Our waiter at dinner tonight told us the fresh strawberries were excellent."

"Oh—thank you—with tea, please." Nancy wasn't hungry in the least, but she was finding Sarah Amberly's company fascinating. She'd been intrigued by her interpretation of the tarot cards.

"Make yourself at home while I order," Sarah told Nancy with a sweeping gesture that seemed to say, "What's mine is yours." Then she picked up the phone.

Nancy wandered over to a series of photos in antique silver frames that stood on the marble fireplace. She recognized Sarah Amberly as a bride, her arm linked with that of a dashing young man in a Panama hat and white suit.

"That's my Joshua," Sarah called from the

phone, while she waited for room service to answer. "That picture was taken on our wedding trip. He was the grandest man who ever lived, dear. There's not another like him, and never will be."

In another photo, the young couple were holding a smiling blond baby. In another, the Amberlys stood with a lanky, black-haired boy, whom Nancy recognized as a young Jack Kale.

"Our only child, Barbara, died when she was three years old. That's her—the blond girl."

Nancy nodded sympathetically. Losing a child had to be one of the worst blows life could deal anyone. Was that why Sarah seemed so lonely?

"The boy in the other photo is Jack Kale, my nephew. When my brother and his wife were killed, we brought Jack to live with us and raised him as our very own son. He was handsome even then. Every little girl wanted to marry him.

"Unfortunately, he was too young to appreciate what we did for him. Ah, but then, that's my Jack, devil-may-care and full of himself. He's good at heart, I suppose. But not half the man his uncle was—" Suddenly her conversation was cut short as she paid attention to the phone.

"Room service? Well, you certainly take your time in answering! Of course this is Mrs. Amberly! I happen to have a lovely young guest and I wish you to send us two orders of strawberries and tea. And I do mean pronto!" Hanging up, Sarah regarded Nancy with a coy smile. "If you don't prod the mules, they will never pull the cart."

For all her charm and friendliness, Sarah certainly had a take-charge personality. Nancy supposed the older woman didn't mean to be rude, but she was awfully definite about what she wanted and when.

"Joshua taught me years ago to be firm with servants. It's better for all concerned," Sarah said as if reading Nancy's mind.

"Who are these little girls?" Nancy held up a photo of two girls, one about fifteen and the other a toddler. They were dressed in ragged clothes. In the background was a dilapidated old house.

"Why, Nancy dear, don't you recognize me?" Sarah Amberly laughed a rich, full laugh. "That photo was taken when my sister Alison and I were living in the north end of Boston. My father worked on the docks, and my mother took in laundry. I met Joshua just a few years after that photo was taken. I was hired as his mother's personal secretary, and he fell in love with me at first sight."

In the photo Sarah looked out boldly, but Alison's eyes avoided the camera; they had a faraway look.

"Poor, poor Alison. Always a nervous child, and now— My mother thought it was because she was born during a thunderstorm, but, of course, that's nonsense.

"Oh, well, I do what I can for her now. I'm all she has, poor thing. And for her I must remain healthy and strong. I fear my nephew would not take very good care of her should anything happen to me."

It was while Sarah was speaking that Nancy first noticed the ring through the open door in Sarah's bedroom. It was lying on a small table next to her bed. The gleam from the lamp above it struck the ring in a way that sent a shower of rosy rainbows all over the bedroom.

"Oh, my. What a beautiful piece of jewelry!" Nancy exclaimed, almost in spite of herself. "The one on your bedside table."

"Ah—you like rubies! Run in and bring it out to me, please." Sarah took the ring lovingly in her fingers. "My engagement ring. It once belonged to Abigail Amberly, Joshua's great-grandmother. Before that, the stone was a crown jewel of an Ottoman ruler.

"Joshua was born to great wealth, you see. But he took a successful family business and turned it into an international corporation. That's the kind of person he was. . . ." As she recalled her husband, Sarah almost looked like a young woman again. It was as if she were in another world.

Abruptly she snapped herself out of her reverie.

"Unfortunately, my arthritis has swollen my finger too much for me to wear the ruby anymore. But I always keep it beside my bed wherever I travel. Somehow, when the ring is near me, I can almost imagine that Joshua is with me, too. Do you find that strange?"

"No, not really," Nancy answered, touched by the woman's deep emotion. Obviously, Sarah Amberly was not the cold and cranky person she had first appeared to be. She was warm, smart, and wonderfully offbeat.

"If Joshua were here now, he'd be furious with the way things are turning out. Simply furious." Sarah's whole mood seemed to turn and her face clouded over.

"My nephew is throwing my money away as fast as he can take it from me. Alison, poor Alison, in her condition— Oh, when I think of what may lie ahead, I feel as if I'm on a collision course with destiny, and everything is reeling out of control. Look at this!"

Turning over the tarot cards that were arranged like a wheel around the first one, Sarah muttered, "The Three of Cups was the only bright spot. All the others—ghastly cards. When Madame Rosa read me this afternoon, I felt suddenly so afraid. Everything she was saying was pointing to the most horrible—"

"Why, Sarah! You're up!" The man's voice at the front door was cool and crisp. He walked into the room, and Nancy recognized him as Sarah's companion, the distinguished middle-aged man. He smiled, walked up to Sarah, and touched her tenderly on the shoulder. "Darling," he said softly.

"Oh, hello, Pieter," Sarah replied almost listlessly. Telling Nancy about her tarot reading seemed to have depressed her.

"And who is your young friend?" asked Pieter, politely smiling at Nancy.

"Pieter van Druten, meet Nancy Drew. Pieter, this young lady practically saved my life. I seem to have mislaid my tablets, and she found me at the very last moment."

"Thank goodness you were near, Miss Drew." Pieter van Druten extended his hand and smiled tightly at her. Nancy felt a cold shiver go through her when she returned his grasp.

"She was magnificent, Pieter. The Three of Cups personified."

"Yes, I'm sure. Miss Drew, is there anything further you'll be needing?"

Nancy understood that Pieter was trying to hurry her out of the Amberly suite. And in his tone she picked up a kind of disdain for the tarot cards, too.

Just then a knock was heard.

"Are you expecting anyone, Sarah?" Pieter wanted to know.

"Yes, room service. Let them in."

Pieter walked to the door and opened it. "You may put that down here," he ordered the waiter, pointing to the coffee table.

Nancy nodded when she saw Maximilian enter the room. "Good evening," he murmured politely to Nancy and Sarah.

"Now, now, just leave our order and be on your way," Pieter said coolly. "Nobody pays you to stay and chat."

Maybe he was making a joke, but if he was, Nancy thought it was a poor one. Pieter's whole attitude was so superior, so cold. Nancy saw pure hatred burning in Maximilian's eyes as he nodded to Pieter and obediently left the room.

"I'm sorry to have to break up this lovely visit, but I really must discuss an urgent matter with Mrs. Amberly in private." So saying, Pieter grasped Nancy gently but firmly by the elbow and led her to the door. Nancy turned to see Sarah's reaction, but the woman merely nodded listlessly.

"Oh, dear, if this is about Jack, I'm not sure I want to hear it," she murmured.

Pieter van Druten turned to Nancy with a humorless smile. "I'm sure you understand, Miss Drew. Good night."

And before Nancy could even say good night to her new friend, the door was slammed behind her.

"Well, it's nearly nine A.M.—hope your meetings aren't too boring today, Dad." Nancy got up from their breakfast table at the Palm Court to kiss her father goodbye. "See you around four?"

"Let's hope so," said Carson doubtfully. "You know how meetings are. But whatever happens, we've got dinner at the Russian Tea Room tonight, and theater tickets for that matinee tomorrow—don't forget."

"Don't worry, I won't." Nancy laughed. "How many Tony Awards did it win? Ten?"

Carson waved as he walked off, his leather briefcase in hand. Nancy was about to sit back down and drink another cup of tea when she spotted Sarah Amberly walking down the lobby hallway on the other side of the palms. Nancy was surprised. The night before Sarah had seemed so ill, yet here she was out of her room.

Quickly, Nancy went around the palms and caught up with her. "Hi!" she called with a big smile.

But Sarah Amberly acted as if she barely recognized her. "Oh— Oh, yes— Hello, there . . ."

It was as if the night before hadn't even happened! Sarah's face was troubled, anxious, and her eyes kept darting around, as if she were expecting something extremely unpleasant.

"Is everything all right?" Nancy couldn't help asking, reaching out to the older woman.

"Oh, it's nothing—nothing. I've just come from Madame Rosa's—"

"Another tarot reading? But I thought she came up to your suite."

Again Sarah Amberly looked around warily.

31

"Yes, normally she does. It's just, you know, more—private this way."

"Well, did she have anything new to say?" Nancy asked. What could Madame Rosa possibly have said that had upset Sarah so much?

"No, nothing really. Excuse me, please. I just can't . . . talk about it."

Slowly the woman turned and walked down the corridor, wringing her hands absent-mindedly.

Nancy was dumbfounded. What had happened to change things so drastically?

Just then a man darted out from behind a palm and took off down the corridor in the direction Sarah Amberly had gone. Nancy recognized him as Maximilian the waiter.

He was following Sarah! But why? Did he have some sinister purpose in mind? Events surrounding Sarah Amberly were becoming stranger and stranger! Nancy couldn't shake the feeling that Sarah Amberly was in some sort of big trouble. And if she was, Nancy had to help her.

She started off after them at a rapid pace. But just as she rounded the first corner, a pair of hands reached out and grabbed her. Before Nancy could scream, her mouth and eyes were covered, and she felt herself being pulled backward!

Chapter

Four

DON'T MOVE—OR else!"

Nancy was released, and she wheeled around to face her assailant. Instead she found herself staring into the laughing eyes of her two best friends, Bess Marvin and George Fayne.

"Bess! George! What are you two doing here!" The relief Nancy felt was tinged with disappointment. Something told her that if she'd followed Maximilian she might have gained a little more information about what was going on in the Amberly suite. Still, it was great to see her friends standing there in the corridor of the Plaza!

"Surprise!" Bess gave her friend a quick hug. "I told you we couldn't let you come to New York without us!" Bess gushed.

"Bess actually talked both of our mothers into sending us here." George shook her head happily, her short, dark hair dancing. Despite her nickname of George, Georgia Fayne was one hundred percent female.

"It's true. I was brilliant." Bess laughed, her pretty face lighting up with glee. "I convinced them that we needed to broaden our cultural horizons."

"She didn't mention shopping, of course—" George added, referring to one of Bess's favorite activities.

"Then when I told her that *you* were here with your father, Nan—well, that cinched it. And here we are!"

"Fantastic!" Looking at Bess and George's smiling faces made Nancy grin, too. She'd just have to catch up to Maximilian some other time.

"Where are you staying?" Nancy asked.

Bess's nose wrinkled up as she twisted a strand of her glossy blond hair. *"Not* here at the Plaza, unfortunately."

"Alas," quipped George. "We're in more humble quarters."

"But it does have color TV—" Bess said.

"And an ice pitcher—" George laughed.

"But it's *not,* repeat, *not,* the Plaza." Bess

34

sighed. "I'm overcome with jealousy just thinking about your staying here."

"Oh gosh, it really is great to see you!" Nancy couldn't help feeling better. After all the weird things she'd been finding out about the Amberly party, Bess and George were just what she needed—nice normal friends!

"So, what's happening around the Big Apple, Nan? Any interesting guys?" With Bess, it was always the same question: Where are the boys?

"Come on now, Bess," chided George, "Nancy's got a boyfriend, remember."

"Oh, don't be so serious, George. After all, Nancy's allowed to look," Bess said, defending herself.

Nancy smiled. "Well, as a matter of fact, there is a pretty cute guy staying in the suite right next to ours."

"Oh?" said Bess, throwing her arm around her friend's shoulder as they walked through the lobby. "Is that cute as in blond—or dark?"

"Dark," murmured Nancy. "And cute doesn't really say it. Incredibly handsome is more like it."

"But there's something about him you don't trust," George said. "You're frowning."

Nancy smiled—she could never hide anything from George. "Am I frowning? Well, I'm not sure about the guy, but the main thing is, something very weird is going on in that suite where he's staying."

"Uh-huh—and?"

"It's his aunt—she's one of the Amberly family. You know, of Boston?"

Two blank stares met her gaze. "Tell us all about it over some shopping," said Bess, tugging at her arm. "You could use some new clothes, girl. After all, you're staying at the Plaza!"

"Hey! What are you doing? I was right in the middle of something—"

Nancy knew it was no use. Sarah and Maximilian were long gone; she'd never catch up to them now. And George and Bess were right there.

"So what do you think?" Nancy was browsing through the racks at Saks, one of New York's poshest department stores, but her mind was on Sarah Amberly. She'd told Bess and George everything that had happened in the suite next door.

"Isn't it creepy?" she asked. "I'm really worried about Sarah Amberly. All around her things are so weird—hateful notes, stealing, pills placed out of her reach . . . What do you two think? Any brilliant ideas?"

Bess shot Nancy a quick look and said, "*I* think that peach outfit you just flipped by is the ultimate, and if you're really serious about getting yourself something incredible to wear, you've *got* to try it on."

With a sigh, George took Nancy by the shoulder. "Okay, Drew—I'm going to break it to you gently. You really need a vacation."

"Huh?" Nancy frowned.

"She's right, Nancy," Bess put in. "We've decided you're taking things too seriously. You came to New York to have a good time, remember? And now you're all wound up about this Amberly thing. I mean, there doesn't *always* have to be a mystery going on. Maybe you're reading things into this that really aren't there."

Surprised by Bess's opinion, Nancy turned to George.

"It's true, Nancy," George said softly. "You know, you don't want to go off the deep end over every little thing." It wasn't often George would say something like that, so Nancy had to listen.

"But there *is* something going on here—I can just feel it," Nancy protested.

Bess looked skeptical. "Even if there is, what's the difference? When are you going to take some time for *yourself* and have a little fun?"

"I have tons of fun!" Nancy argued, a little too fiercely. But then she had to wonder if George and Bess weren't telling her the truth the way nobody else would. Maybe she *was* taking life too seriously these days.

"Size six! Perfect. And only a million dollars!" Bess said, fingering the label of the peach ensemble. The three girls caught one another's eyes and cracked up.

"Well, my dad did say to buy something new," Nancy said. With a sly smile, and a vow to forget about Sarah Amberly, Nancy walked into the dressing room.

She emerged a few minutes later, wearing the soft peach wool skirt and jacket and an ivory silk blouse. The whole outfit set off her coloring perfectly. Even Nancy knew she looked terrific.

"It's fabulous," said George.

"Smashing!" Bess agreed.

"Sold," said Nancy. A short while later, having changed back to her street clothes and paid for the outfit, Nancy stepped out onto Fifth Avenue, feeling renewed and refreshed. The box from Saks was under her arm, and her friends were at her side.

"Oh, I love New York!" Bess cried out a bit later as they stood at the corner of Fifth Avenue and Fifty-seventh Street, waiting for the light to turn green. "Can't you just feel the electricity in the air?"

"Makes River Heights seem pretty dull, actually," George agreed with a wistful sigh.

"Look! There's Tiffany's! We've *got* to check it out. Come on!" Bess headed straight for the famous jewelry store, tugging on Nancy's sleeve.

In the window was a glittering array of precious jewels that caught the midday sun and reflected it back.

"Can you believe the size of that ruby?" Bess

exclaimed, pointing to a gem set in a gold necklace.

"Sarah Amberly's is twice that size," Nancy said, waiting for Bess's reaction.

With a gasp, Bess turned to her friend. "You're kidding—right?"

"No, I'm not kidding. It really is. I saw it last night."

"Now, that's the first interesting thing you've said about the Amberlys since we got here. Any chance of getting a peek at it?"

"I can't promise, but I'll try to introduce you to Sarah." The thought of another visit to the Amberly suite sounded good to Nancy. Not that she was going to get involved—George and Bess had convinced her to leave things alone just this once in her life. Still, it couldn't hurt to check in with Sarah, just to see how she was doing.

"But we've got to get you shoes first," Bess asserted. "You really should have new ones to go with your outfit."

George reached into her purse and pulled out a piece of paper. "There's this shoe store the flight attendant was telling us about. I have the address right here. Sixty-second and Madison. That's, let's see—northeast from here, I think."

"Remind me to go camping with you sometime, George." Bess laughed, heading uptown behind her cousin.

"Hey, why don't we walk through the park?"

Nancy suggested. A stroll through Central Park with her two best buddies in the entire world would be perfect.

"Great idea!" said Bess.

An hour later, after a walk through Central Park and a quick stop at the shoe store, where Nancy picked out a stylish pair of Italian pumps, the trio found themselves strolling down Sixty-second Street.

"Oh, Nancy—don't you wish you could buy that topaz necklace we saw in Tiffany's window? It would be so terrific with the—Nan? Nan?"

Nancy wasn't paying attention. Her eyes were riveted on the far end of the block, where Alison Kale had just emerged from the front door of a stately old brownstone. As the girls watched, Alison walked right by them, muttering to herself.

"Whoa!" gasped George when Alison was out of earshot. "Just a little bizarre—"

"That's Sarah Amberly's sister," Nancy said softly.

George let out a low whistle. "Now I see why you're worried about Mrs. Amberly. She's surrounded by thieves and weirdos."

Nancy smiled triumphantly. "Still think I need a vacation?"

After Alison passed, the girls walked to the brownstone she'd come from and read the shingle hanging outside: Dr. Arnold Mitchell, Psychiatric Specialist.

"So, she's under a psychiatrist's care," said Nancy. "That's good to know."

"She looks like she really needs it, too," Bess murmured sympathetically as they headed back to the Plaza.

"Do you think Mrs. Amberly will really let us see the ruby?" Bess asked when they stepped off the elevator on the top floor, their feet sinking into the plush forest green carpet.

"I can't be sure," Nancy answered. "Yesterday she was very friendly, but today when I saw her again she seemed awfully distracted. Here's her suite."

"Sarah? Mrs. Amberly?" Nancy rapped on the door, and the girls waited. No answer. "I wonder," murmured Nancy. She reached down and jiggled the doorknob. The latch clicked open.

"That door is unlocked, Nancy!" George exclaimed.

"I hope Sarah's all right. Maybe she's in there and can't answer," Nancy said with a worried look.

"Well, in that case—" George tapped the door lightly, and it opened. The three girls looked at one another and then walked in, closing the door behind them.

"Hello. Sarah? Are you here?" Nancy called as she made her way into Sarah's bedroom.

"Wow! What a place!" Bess gasped.

But the bedroom was empty. "Come on, let's go. You can meet her later—" Nancy started to say. But as she turned to leave, she noticed that Sarah's ruby ring was gone from the little table beside the bed.

"That's odd—Sarah said she always kept her ring by her bed," Nancy said.

Just then, two men appeared in the doorway of the bedroom, and Nancy, Bess, and George jumped.

"All right—step right over to the wall and put your hands over your heads!" a harsh voice commanded. "You're all under arrest!"

Chapter

Five

SPINNING AROUND BREATHLESSLY, Nancy found herself looking into the eyes of a fair-haired young man of about twenty-five. He held a security man's badge in one hand and a pistol in the other. Behind him, his lanky assistant stared at the three girls, his mouth wide open. "Three girls . . ." the assistant murmured.

"You never know who's a thief, Felske," the fair-haired man muttered. Then he waved his pistol and barked, "Okay, ladies. Move it."

"Wait a minute," Nancy spoke up. "We weren't doing anything wrong—and you haven't got a shred of evidence that says we were."

43

With a smile, the young man put his badge away, but he kept the pistol aimed at Nancy and her friends. "Sure, sure. That line may have worked other places, sweetie, but this is the Plaza. You just got caught in one of the finest security nets in the world. I'm Joe Ritter, staff detective here. Now, if you'll all come with me. The New York police are looking for people like you."

"But she's telling the truth!" cried Bess, the first glint of tears pooling in her eyes. "We *weren't* doing anything wrong!"

"Sure, sure. Come along, now." He motioned to them with the pistol. "Tell that to the judge."

Well, Nancy thought. It did look bad. They were in someone else's room without permission. At that moment Sarah Amberly appeared at the door to the bedroom. A bolt of relief shot through Nancy like lightning.

"What is the meaning of this intrusion, young man!" she shouted. "Nancy, did he hurt you?"

"No, they've just misunderstood what's going on here—" Nancy was about to explain everything when Sarah's eyes fell to the little table.

"My ruby! It's gone!"

"We happened to be patrolling the hall when we saw these trespassers, Mrs. Amberly. Okay, girls—where's the ring?"

"Sarah, I came in because I thought you might be ill again," Nancy explained. "The ring was gone when we got here."

44

"We never even saw it, honestly!" Bess cried.

"Oh, I never thought he would sink so low," Sarah murmured, letting herself down onto the bed. "Never, never . . ."

Nancy wondered if "he" was Jack Kale. Something in the woman's sad face told her it might be.

"Would you like to press charges now or later, Mrs. Amberly?" the blond young man asked. "We'll work at your convenience."

"Press charges? Against whom?" A kind of confused irritation passed over Sarah's face.

"Why, the perpetrators! These three!" He was still waving his pistol at them.

"Oh, dear me, no," Sarah answered with a small laugh. "Not now or later. This young lady," she said, indicating Nancy, "was sent to me by an authority higher than hotel security. She is my protectress, and I have already given her permission to visit my suite at any time. Besides, she is a guest at this hotel."

Joe Ritter frowned. Nancy could tell he was thinking that Sarah Amberly was slightly crazy. "Yes, but your ring," he countered gingerly. "It *is* missing, isn't it?"

"Yes, yes. But I'm quite sure I know who has it, and I'd prefer to handle it myself. You and your assistant are free to go now."

Detective Ritter stared blankly at Sarah for a minute before he headed for the door. "Come on,

Felske," he muttered, shooting Nancy an angry look.

When they were gone, Sarah gave Nancy a warm smile. "Nancy, who are your friends?"

"This is Bess Marvin and George Fayne—my two best friends from back home."

"How do you do, girls? Will you promise to come back another time when I can be more hospitable? I'm afraid that ruby means a great deal to me, and I want to organize my thoughts so I can get it back—if it's not too late."

Nancy met the older woman's eyes with a sympathetic frown. "Sarah, maybe my friends and I can help you get your ring back," she offered gently. "I know how much it means to you."

"Oh, no. No, dear. But thank you for the offer. It's a family matter, that's all," she replied with as much dignity as she could muster. "Now, if you'll excuse me."

"Of course," Bess said, and George nodded.

"I'm so sorry for the intrusion, Sarah," Nancy apologized. "I hope you don't mind my coming into the suite that way—"

Sarah Amberly reached out and took Nancy's hand. She pressed it warmly. "There is no need to apologize, Nancy. I trust your judgment, and I assure you, you are always welcome in here, my dear. After all, we were fated to be friends, weren't we? However, I am greatly distressed by this latest piece of mischief." With that, her thoughts seemed to turn inward. Nancy knew it was time to leave.

"Well, if you need anything, remember I'm right next door," Nancy said, touching Sarah's bony shoulder gently before she left.

Stepping outside, the girls were surprised to find a smoldering Joe Ritter waiting for them. He looked at Nancy with a scowl that could break a mirror. "Listen, I'm letting you go this time. But don't try anything funny from here on in— understand?"

Nancy's eyes met his, but he glanced away. Sure, things looked suspicious to Ritter. But there was no way she was going to convince him of her innocent intentions. He'd never believe her. "Let's go," she said to her friends.

None of the girls said a word as Nancy led them back to her suite; they were still too shaken to speak. But once they made it safely inside, Bess started to giggle. Soon Nancy and George were smiling, and then all three of them burst out laughing as the humor of the situation struck them.

Sprawled around the luxurious suite, they recalled the details of their near arrest and broke up completely.

"Hey! Let's call room service and order a cake with a file baked inside. We may need it," Bess said, cracking herself up.

"I guess we really did look guilty, didn't we?" George commented.

"Honestly, we did," Nancy said. "He was right to stop us—maybe his methods were a little too harsh, though."

"Come on, Nan," Bess said. "Let's not get all serious."

"Well, some things *are* serious, Bess," Nancy said. "Whether you believe it or not."

"You know what I think is serious?" Bess was no longer laughing. "The last time you came to New York and you almost got *killed*. Just be sure to be careful—okay?"

Silence fell for a long minute.

"Hey, lighten up, you two," George finally commanded.

"I get worried about you, that's all!" said Bess, her affection shining in her eyes.

"Me, too, Nan," George nodded.

Nancy looked from one friend to the other. "Oh, come on, you two." She playfully tossed a peach satin pillow at Bess. "I mean, this is really dangerous, right? Here I am at the Plaza—I'm having the time of my life with my best friends and stuffing my face with éclairs. Somehow it doesn't seem too dangerous to me!" Nancy's blue eyes sparkled mischievously now.

"All right, all right. Just take care of yourself, okay?" said Bess cheerfully.

"Listen," Nancy suggested, "my dad is going to be back from the convention any minute, and we have a dinner date—want to come along? I know he'd love to see you."

George slumped down into her chair. "Oh, I wish we could! But Bess and I have big plans, don't we, Bess?"

Bess laughed. "We promised to visit my mom's ex-roommate on the Upper West Side. I call her Aunt Julie. She's cooking up a storm for us."

Nancy nodded. "Hey! I have an idea—why don't we get together after dinner? I know my dad is going to want to turn in early. The three of us could check out the nightlife at the Trump Tower."

"Yeah! Maybe talk to some real-life New York City guys," Bess exclaimed. "What do you say, George?"

George nodded. "See you about when, Nan?"

"Oh, I don't know—eight-thirty, quarter to nine?"

"You're on," said George on the way out.

"See you later!" Bess called from the hall.

Alone, Nancy took out her new outfit and held it up in front of the mirror. It still looked great. She was admiring it when suddenly she heard a shout from behind the wall that adjoined the Amberly suite.

Angry voices followed. Sarah Amberly's booming tones and a man's—Jack Kale's, maybe? But what were they saying? All Nancy could hear were muffled shouts. The argument must have been taking place in the main room of the Amberly suite, not in Sarah's bedroom.

Nancy clenched her fists in frustration. She

was worried about Sarah. If only she could hear what they were saying and knew that Sarah was all right.

Thinking quickly, she went to the window and threw it open. She leaned out as far as she safely could and twisted her body to the left, the better to hear the sound from around the side of the gabled window.

Sure enough, the voices were clearer now. The Amberlys' windows were open, just as they had been whenever Nancy was in their suite.

"You're a devil, that's what you are!" Sarah shouted. "What did Joshua and I ever deny you, that you repay me this way?"

"Hold on, Aunt Sarah" was the angry reply. "How do you know it was me who stole it? Maybe it was your precious beau—oh, no, I forgot, he never does *anything* wrong, does he?"

"Look to your own faults, young man!" Sarah yelled back at him. "I've given you everything—everything!"

"Now, now, Aunt Sarah. I may triple your wealth one of these days. I only hope you're not in the great hereafter when I hit it big at the gaming tables."

"You'd like that, wouldn't you?" Nancy could tell from the shaking in her voice that Sarah Amberly was hurt to the quick.

"I should have taken a firmer stand with you a long time ago, young man, but you've had me

50

wrapped around your little finger, haven't you? Well, it's not too late. I'll fix you—I'll cut you out of my will. Then you'll have to learn to work for a living. I'll teach you the value of a dollar yet!"

"You won't disinherit me, Aunt Sarah—you know you won't. Uncle Joshua made you promise on his deathbed, remember?"

Nancy leaned a little farther out the window to hear better. Sarah and Jack had turned toward the far wall and the sound wasn't traveling as well.

"Devil! You devil! Your uncle is turning in his grave, I'm sure," said Sarah Amberly. "And I *will* disinherit you, don't think I won't. If that ring isn't back on this table by tomorrow, I'm calling my lawyer!"

"You'll never do it, Aunt Sarah" was the young man's reply. "Never." Nancy drew her breath in sharply. She heard a door slam and then silence.

Whew! Nancy thought. She was glad now she had listened in, nosy as it might have seemed. Sarah Amberly *was* in real danger, she felt it in her bones. But what could she *do* about it? How could she help?

Preoccupied, Nancy started to draw her head back in. But as she did so, she banged her head—hard—against the bottom of the window.

She felt a throbbing, and heard a ringing noise. It lasted only a fraction of a second, but in that amount of time, she lost her balance and felt herself start to slip. Her arms flailed wildly, grasping at the empty air.

She couldn't even scream. There was no time for that. Below her was the street, thirty stories down—and she was going over the ledge to land on it.

Chapter
Six

IN THE LAST split second left to her, with an extra ounce of strength from somewhere deep inside, Nancy threw her head up and twisted herself around, reaching back with her fingertips.

There! She grabbed the window and pushed herself inside, collapsing in a terrified heap on the floor. She'd been lucky this time, and she knew it. Mighty lucky. She lay there, breathing in deep drafts of air. I'm still alive! was all she could think.

But when the relief subsided, and she picked herself up off the carpet, she muttered, "You idiot!" Leaning so far out the window had been incredibly dumb.

Maybe she was being overzealous. After all, the only crime that had been committed was a theft, and Sarah Amberly had insisted on handling that herself. The loss of the jewel was hardly something to die for.

After walking to the mirror, Nancy smoothed her hair and looked down at her hands, which were raw and scratched from her close call at the window. Then she checked her watch. She was startled to realize it was almost time for dinner.

She went to the closet door and pulled the peach skirt from its hanger. Just then, her father popped his head inside. Carson's face was tired and strained.

"Hi, Dad!" she called. "You look bushed."

Carson nodded and sighed. "That's one way to put it. Between the speeches and the heavy lunch I feel like I'm made of lead. How was your day, Nancy?"

"I got a new outfit today. In fact, I thought I'd wear it tonight for our big dinner—"

"Honey, about that dinner . . ."

The moment the words were out of his mouth, Nancy knew what was coming next.

"Nan, would you mind very much if we did it tomorrow instead? I was thinking maybe we could order from room service tonight—but only if that's okay with you."

Looking at her father's weary face, Nancy couldn't make him push himself any more than he already had.

"Room service sounds like fun, actually," she said, hanging up her new outfit again. At least they'd have the whole next day and Sunday. Now that her dad's meetings were over, they could really spend some time together.

Nancy had to blink when she read the prices on the room service menu, but Carson insisted she order whatever she wanted. Half an hour later there was a knock on the door, and Maximilian appeared behind a rolling silver table.

What *is* it about him? Nancy wondered. The waiter cast a sickening smile in their direction.

"Lobster à la maison for two? Asparagus almondine in sherry sauce?" he asked.

"That's us," Carson said.

"And I have a bottle of sparkling water?"

"Yup," said Carson. "That's us, too."

"How are you, miss?" Maximilian inquired as he rolled the cart in front of the sofa and began setting up for dinner.

"Fine, thank you," Nancy answered politely. She couldn't decide how she felt about this man.

Carson left the room to get tip money. Suddenly Maximilian leaned toward Nancy, speaking in hushed tones. "I probably shouldn't mention it, miss, but if you have any jewelry, you might consider putting it in the hotel safe. There was a robbery on this floor today."

"Oh?" Nancy asked innocently.

"There's a young man next door who loves money more than life," he continued. "But then, perhaps you already know about it—"

"Actually, Mrs. Amberly did mention it to me." She wouldn't give him more than that. Let him tell her what he knew. And Maximilian knew something. Nancy could just bet on it. Something vital.

"I understand you, er, fell under suspicion? Most regrettable. The young Ritter, he is bull-headed, yes?" Now the waiter gave her a leering smile.

Just then, Carson came back. "Here you go," he said lightly, handing Maximilian the tip.

Nancy watched the waiter roll the cart from the room, the same smirk on his face. What was it that he knew?

"What's wrong, honey?"

"Oh, nothing, Dad." Nancy sat at the small marble table and looked over at her father with a wan smile. There was no sense telling him all the things she was thinking—everything was still so jumbled.

"Your hands, Nancy! What happened to them?"

Nancy looked at the scrape marks, then quickly put her hands under the table. "Oh, nothing," she murmured. "I was just closing the window and it got stuck."

Ordinarily, Nancy would never fib to her father, but this time she was afraid to tell him the truth. If he knew how close she'd come to real harm, he'd be very upset.

"Oh—I forgot to tell you, Dad. George and Bess are in town! I'm meeting them at Trump Tower tonight!" Nancy picked up her fork.

Carson gave her an amused look. "George and Bess, eh? What do you know." He looked at her fingertips again. "Want me to break up your lobster for you?" he asked with a little smile.

"Thanks, Dad. I guess you'd better."

"The window got stuck, huh?"

A few hours later Nancy was sipping cappuccino with George and Bess at a café overlooking the Trump Tower atrium. Around them gleamed some of New York's most chic stores.

"Isn't this fantastic?" she asked. Bess and George agreed.

Nearby, waterfalls cascaded from a hidden source within the burnished marble walls of Trump Tower into glittering pools below. Somewhere, a flute and cello played something that sounded like Bach.

Nancy finshed a bite of anisette toast and looked over at her friends. "So how are you two holding up? Long day?"

"Aunt Julie's pot roast did me in," George admitted. "If only I hadn't let her talk me into seconds . . ."

"Well then, what do you say we get together again after the matinee tomorrow? My dad and I are going to see *Music!* and then we're having dinner someplace really special. Maybe you can come. Afterward, we could catch a cab to Greenwich Village and go to a jazz club or something—"

"Sounds good, Nan," said Bess as they paid the check and headed down the escalator.

They were still discussing plans for the next day when Nancy spotted a familiar figure coming toward them on the up escalator. It was Pieter van Druten. He was holding an airline-ticket folder.

Nancy grabbed her friends and whispered, "Look, that's the guy I told you about—Sarah Amberly's boyfriend."

"Kind of old," said Bess nonchalantly.

Nancy turned to watch as van Druten stepped off the escalator and into an exclusive men's store. He looked so self-satisfied, so casual, his lips permanently pursed in a nasty little smile.

"Listen, would you mind if we waited outside

and followed him?" Nancy found herself saying. "I'm kind of interested—"

"Nancy Drew, you're hopeless," said George with a shake of her head. "Okay, let's go."

They trailed Pieter van Druten to the lobby of the Plaza, where he entered the dry-cleaning shop, which was open until midnight. The girls watched from across the hall as he dropped off a shirt he had been carrying inside his jacket. He soon emerged and walked on.

"Bess, George—you keep following van Druten. I'm going to see if I can get that shirt back."

"Okay," Bess said. "But this is absolutely it for tonight." She and George headed in the same direction that van Druten had gone.

By the time Nancy had retrieved the shirt, Bess and George were waiting for her.

"Where's van Druten?" Nancy asked.

"He's having a late supper in one of the restaurants," George replied. "We figured he'd be there awhile, so we decided to come back."

"What did you want the shirt for, anyway?" Bess asked.

"Just a hunch," Nancy said, stuffing it in her purse. "Thanks for all your help, guys."

"Well, good night, Nancy. Talk to you tomorrow," George said.

Nancy headed back to her suite. As soon as she

stepped off the elevator she knew something was wrong—desperately wrong. Every fiber in her being tensed.

The Amberlys' door was open—wide open. That's odd, thought Nancy.

She peered inside. She saw no one, and was about to leave, when she heard a sound that made her blood run cold. It was a sort of throaty rattling. The source of the sound was definitely human, and whoever was making it was in deep trouble.

Running into Sarah's bedroom, Nancy saw the older woman. Sarah had fallen off the bed and was grasping the empty air, her eyes wild with pain and terror. The bottle of pills was on the floor, and the pills themselves scattered around. The water glass lay shattered nearby, as did a teacup and saucer.

"Sarah! Are you all right?" Nancy asked. "What's happened?" She took the woman in her arms and was surprised to feel how cold she was, as if she'd been bathing in ice water.

"Th—Kkk—Aaa—"

Nancy couldn't make out what Sarah was saying, but she knew it must be terribly important. The woman seemed to be imploring her to listen. Nancy leaned in closer, her ear practically on her lips.

"Th—Dev—ev—vil—" Sarah was saying now. "Th—th—fff—foo—ool—"

Sarah seemed to grow rigid in Nancy's arms. "And—and—D-D—eee—eath-th," she gasped. Again came the hideous rattling, and then she went limp.

"No! No!" shouted Nancy. "I won't let you die!" Nancy seized the older woman and pounded on her chest rhythmically, desperately trying to get her breathing again.

But it was too late. Sarah Amberly was already dead.

Chapter

Seven

I CAN'T BELIEVE it. She just didn't respond. Nothing I tried was any use." Nancy looked up at her father, her large blue eyes filled with agony and self-doubt. They were standing with the manager of the hotel in the main room of the Amberly suite, waiting for the hotel doctor to arrive. "For all the good I did, I might as well not have even been here."

"Nancy, Nancy—you did everything you could. No one can work miracles." Carson Drew patted his daughter's shoulder tenderly and drew her toward him.

"But I let her down, Dad. I did. I just . . . just—oh, I felt so helpless."

"You did everything you possibly could."

Just then a white-haired man in a dark suit entered the suite. From the black leather bag he was carrying, Nancy guessed he must be the doctor.

"Where's Mrs. Amberly?" he asked.

"In there." The manager pointed to Sarah's bedroom. He and the doctor went in, Carson and Nancy following behind.

Seeing Sarah so still on the floor, her face twisted into an expression of pained surprise, made Nancy wince. Why hadn't she found a way to save her?

"Hmmm . . ." the doctor murmured, finishing his examination. Then, turning to Nancy, he asked, "You're the young lady who reported this?"

"Yes."

"And when was it exactly?"

"No more than ten minutes ago. I heard a strange sound from the hall. It sounded like she was choking. And when I got here, she was having difficulty breathing. I tried CPR, but she just—" Nancy shivered as she remembered the whole horrible episode.

"No, no," the doctor murmured, with a gentle shake of his head. "You musn't blame yourself. CPR doesn't always work. In fact, I believe Mrs.

Amberly may have died from an overdose of her heart medicine."

With a sigh, he turned back to the body. "I'm afraid this was an act of suicide, and there's nothing you or I or anyone could have done to prevent it. Mrs. Amberly was an unhappy woman, and that coupled with her failing health . . . Well, who knows? Sad, very sad." With that, he gently closed Sarah Amberly's pale eyes and drew the sheet over her face.

"Suicide? But she was *fighting* for her life, doctor. I was here—I saw her!" said Nancy incredulously.

The doctor raised his eyebrows and took Nancy in with a look of gentle wisdom. "My dear, I attended both Mrs. Amberly and her sister many times during their visits here at the Plaza. I assure you, she was fully aware of the consequences of overmedication. Fully aware."

Nancy shook her head sadly. Just half an hour ago she'd been in a glittering café, having fun with George and Bess. If only she'd known what was happening in the Amberly suite!

Suddenly there was a bloodcurdling scream in the outer room. "Where is she? Don't hide her from me!"

Alison Kale burst into the room, followed by two attendants from the hotel staff.

"Sarah! Sarah!" she cried. "What did that monster do to you! What did he do to you?"

"Now, now, calm down, Alison. Try to get hold of yourself," the doctor said.

"Miss Kale, I assure you, the doctor did everything he could," said the hotel manager.

"She was murdered! My sister was murdered!" Alison screamed.

"All right! Everyone just remain calm!" Nancy looked up in time to see Joe Ritter stride into the room, his notebook in hand. "Don't touch anything! Now, would you tell us exactly what happened, doctor? I want to make a full report."

"I'm afraid Mrs. Amberly took an overdose of her heart medication," the doctor began. But he didn't get a chance to finish, because just then Pieter van Druten appeared at the door.

"What's going on here?" he cried, pushing Ritter and the doctor aside. He knelt down next to the bed and pulled back the sheet that covered Sarah's face. "Sarah! My God!" He went rigid for a moment, as if stunned, then bent forward and regarded the dead woman. "Poor darling," he muttered, "her heart finally gave out—"

"Hold it a minute!" Ritter barked. "Don't touch anything! Who are you anyway?"

"I am Pieter van Druten. I was Mrs. Amberly's —fiancé."

"You're lying!" Alison shrieked. "She never promised to marry you. Never!"

Nancy watched Pieter van Druten stand up a little straighter. "We were to be married in six months," he informed the brash young detective with a sad smile. Then, turning to the doctor, he murmured, "It was her heart, wasn't it?"

"I believe it may have been an overdose of her medication, Mr. van Druten," the doctor explained.

"Oh, no. That's quite impossible. Sarah was very careful about her dosage," said van Druten. "Very careful."

"Sarah! Sarah!" Nancy turned around in time to see Alison Kale rush up and grab her sister's body, as if trying to shake it back to life. "How could you leave me alone like this!" the bereft woman shrieked.

"She's hysterical," van Druten said. "Can't you do something, doctor? She may hurt herself."

The doctor nodded and quietly opened his bag.

"You promised you wouldn't—you promised!" Alison continued to rant until the doctor's soothing words did their work.

"There, there, dear. You've had a shock, but you'll feel better soon." He helped her into a chair, handing her a glass of water and a pill. "This will help you rest."

He then began explaining to Detective Ritter what he thought must have happened. Ritter made notes in his little book, nodding the whole time, while Pieter van Druten wandered around the room, taking everything in.

"That's strange," he muttered, opening the top drawer of Sarah's carved rosewood bureau.

"What's strange?" sniffed Ritter.

"Sarah's jewelry box. It's missing."

"Missing!" The young detective pounced on this new development like a hungry dog on a bone.

"It was here just before dinner," said van Druten, wrinkling his brow. "I saw it here myself. Those jewels are worth a fortune!"

"I see," said the detective, his eyes flashing. He addressed the small crowd. "All right, folks, in light of this new information, I have to reevaluate the situation. 'hat we have here is apparently not a suicide, but murder!"

A stunned silence filled the room. Then, Ritter spun around and faced Nancy. "I'm told you were with the deceased when she died?"

"Yes. I was," Nancy answered.

"The doctor here tells me that you claimed Mrs. Amberly was fighting for her life right up to the very end, is that right? Doesn't sound like suicide, does it?" Ritter didn't wait for an answer. "And I see there was no forced entry—that means the crime was committed by someone who was known to the deceased."

Ritter focused on Alison Kale, sitting bleary-eyed in the club chair, then he looked over at Carson and Nancy.

"Felske, take a dusting of the victim's fingertips. See if there's any trace of medicine on them." He laughed a humorless laugh. "There won't be, I predict.

"Hmmm—first the missing ruby, now the missing jewel box. Very interesting, don't you agree, Miss Drew? And definitely *not* a suicide. No, I suspect Mrs. Amberly returned to her room to find someone she knew and trusted, in here. But to Mrs. Amberly's surprise, that someone was in the act of stealing her precious jewelry!

"Mrs. Amberly is shocked," Ritter continued, melodramatically acting out his version of the events as he spoke. "She feels betrayed. Quickly she moves to her bedside to phone the hotel police. But that someone is too quick for her. Before Mrs. A. can make the call, that someone spots the pills and forces them down the poor woman's throat!

"There isn't much of a struggle. Poor Mrs. Amberly's heart is broken with the shock of it all—she's a sick woman, remember. When it's all over, the murderer takes the jewels and runs. A nearly perfect crime, Miss Drew—*nearly* perfect.

"*You* were the last person to see Mrs. Amberly alive tonight. Yesterday *you* were here when the ruby ring was missing. Only Mrs. Amberly's intervention saved you from arrest right then and there." Ritter was looking at Nancy with undisguised scorn.

Nancy didn't answer. What was the use? Detective Ritter had already tried her in his mind and found her guilty. "I think I'd like to speak to my lawyer," she said, looking at Carson.

"Take it easy, you're not under arrest—yet. However, I advise you not to leave this hotel without my permission, Miss Drew. That goes for all the Amberly party as well. Felske, when the nephew gets back, fill him in."

He glanced over at the vacant-eyed Alison. "Just a formality, ma'am." Then he looked straight at Nancy. "I think we've already got our murderer."

Chapter

Eight

Lᴇᴛ's ɢᴇᴛ ᴏᴜᴛ of here!" Carson Drew strode powerfully through the door leading to the waiting area of the police station on Fifty-fourth Street and Eighth Avenue. It was two in the morning.

A weary Nancy followed him at a slower pace. Her normally bright blue eyes were dull and red-rimmed, and her peaches-and-cream complexion was stark white.

"I guess that questioning wasn't *so* bad," Nancy said. "The police just wanted me to tell them everything I knew. If it had been up to Ritter, they would have shone a bright light in my eyes."

She laid a hand on her father's arm. "Thanks for being there with me, Dad."

"What are fathers and lawyers for?" Carson said gently. "Come on, let's head back to the hotel and get some sleep." He held open the door to the police station for her. "Taxi!" he yelled as they reached the curb.

A yellow cab pulled up in seconds. Sinking into the vinyl seat, the lights of the city whizzing past, Nancy tried to smile, but it was impossible. "Oh, Dad, I feel like I've botched everything from the word go."

"Nancy! What are you talking about?"

"It's true. I mean, I've totally ruined our trip to New York. Here's this fabulous city, just waiting to be explored, and I've gotten us into a big mess."

Carson Drew shook his head glumly. "Well, I suppose if you hadn't gotten involved in the first place—"

"But, Dad, I *had* to get involved! Somebody had to help that poor woman. I could feel that Sarah Amberly was in danger, I just *knew* it, but I let the whole situation slip through my fingers."

Carson gazed out at the passing city streets before he spoke. "Nancy," he began gently, taking her hand, "I understand that you were concerned for Sarah. But maybe you let your imagination run away with you. After all, a common thief could have stolen those jewels. . . ."

"Oh, come on, Dad, you know better than that. A simple robbery?" Tired as she was, Nancy could feel the fire returning. "Would a robber have known about her heart medicine? No way!"

Carson pursed his lips and nodded. Nancy had a point. "No, a robber couldn't have known . . ."

Of course, thought Nancy, the image of Jack Kale in her mind, there was one thief who did know. . . .

The next morning Nancy was up at eight. The first thing she did was make a quick phone call. Then she threw a little cold water on her face, ran a brush through her hair, applied some makeup, and dressed. By twenty past, she looked as fresh as if she'd had a full night's sleep.

At eight-thirty the phone in the Drew suite rang twice. "Yes?" Nancy said into the receiver.

"Your guest is here, Miss Drew."

"Thank you. Please send her up."

Nancy was waiting by the door when the knock came. She opened it up and saw a well-dressed woman of about forty. The woman had dark hair and piercing blue eyes, set off by lapis earrings. "Sorry to call you so early, Madame Rosa, but I just *had* to see you," Nancy began. "Please come in."

"I understand completely. Certain things cannot wait." The woman walked into the suite, and Nancy could tell that she was taking in every detail.

"Is it a matter of love?" the woman asked, taking her gloves off and putting her jacket down on a chair.

"No, not really. I just— Well, you see, I've never had my cards read, but I heard you were very good."

"Why, thank you. But I am merely an interpreter. It is the cards that show the way." The woman was smiling sincerely now, and Nancy couldn't help liking her.

"Shall we begin, then? I suggest we start with an astrological clock. That will give you a general overview of your life. Perhaps from there we can be more specific. Would you mix the cards, please, and then lay them down in three piles? I want *your* energy in them, not mine."

Madame Rosa handed Nancy a dark blue felt box, tied with a satin ribbon. Nancy opened it and lifted out an oversize deck of tarot cards.

"There are so many," Nancy commented as she shuffled the cards.

"Seventy-eight," the woman replied. "Each an ancient symbol. Now, if you'll hand them back to me—" Her face a study in concentration, Madame Rosa carefully laid the cards down in a circle on the coffee table in front of the sofa.

"In this reading, each card will represent a house of the zodiac. Let's begin here, in the fifth house, which is the house of love and romance." Throwing a smile at Nancy, she lifted a card and turned it over.

73

"Oh, dear," she murmured. Nancy immediately recognized the card from the very first reading of Sarah's that she had seen. The picture was of a man in a boat. He had a sad expression on his face, and he seemed to be rowing away from a distant shore. "The Six of Swords. I'm afraid your love is distant from you. I do not mean emotionally," she said, laughing, "but distant in miles."

She means Ned, Nancy thought, although it could have been a lucky guess.

"And in the sixth house—ah, the King of Cups. He is an older man, near you now—a man who means a great deal to you. He believes in you very deeply, but he's worried about you. He's concerned for your safety—and not without cause."

Dad. Hadn't he just told her the night before that he was worried about her?

"And for your future—the World. That's a card of great challenge. You must take care to protect yourself at all times. The World is a dangerous card, and next to the Chariot as it is, you must be very strong, very strong indeed—oh, dear!"

When she lifted the next card, Madame Rosa's eyes narrowed. Turning to Nancy, she asked gently, "Have you had a disturbing experience lately? The Nine of Swords in your twelfth house would indicate that you have. See how she covers her eyes to shut out a nightmare?"

Wincing, Nancy recalled the feel of Sarah's limp body in her arms. "The devil, the fool, and death." What had Sarah meant?

"I was friendly with Mrs. Amberly," Nancy began softly. "You know, last night—"

"Yes, I know. Her sister called me. I must say, though, I was saddened but not surprised. Once again the cards foresaw it all."

"How? What was that last reading all about?" Nancy was at the heart of her pursuit with the tarot reader. She narrowed her wide blue eyes and waited for Madame Rosa's response.

"I remember her last reading very vividly. The Tower, the card of sudden violence, and the Ten of Swords, two difficult cards, and in combination—well, they are a dreadful combination. And above them the Three of Swords—betrayal by a loved one."

"When I saw her last night, she said something about a devil and a fool—and death . . ."

"That's strange—those particular cards weren't in her last reading."

"You mean, they're all tarot cards?" A funny feeling made its way up Nancy's spine. "What do they mean?"

"Ominous cards, my dear. The Devil is the card of the lie, the putting of sensual pleasure above moral wholeness. The Fool is the card of misguided innocence, of instability. As for the Death card, well, it could mean drastic change, or it could mean death quite literally. Or the cards may also refer to specific people in a person's life. In your reading, for instance, the King of Cups refers to a specific person. Any of the cardinal cards may do that."

Stunned, Nancy leaned back on the divan. The Devil, the Fool, and Death— Yes, it was all coming clearer now.

"Come in." Alison Kale's voice was feeble. Nancy made her way into her suite quietly. She was shocked when she saw Alison. She looked so weak, so fragile and small in the large bed.

"I hope you're feeling better, Miss Kale," said Nancy. "I'm so sorry about your sister." The early morning visit wasn't going to be easy for Nancy. Alison Kale wasn't going to like what she had to ask about, not one bit.

"Miss Kale, I hope what I'm going to say won't upset you. It's about a piece of paper—a piece of paper I found in this suite—in fact, in this very room. The words 'Kill, Kill, Kill' were written on it."

Alison Kale flushed a deep purple, and suddenly she sat straight up in her bed. "You little snoop!"

"You wrote those words, didn't you, Miss Kale?" Nancy's own heart was pounding now. "And I need to know what you meant by them."

"I—I wrote them because—because my doctor told me to."

"Your *doctor?*" Nancy was puzzled.

"He suggested I could release my feelings freely on paper, if I let myself write what I wanted to. But I never hurt anyone! Never!" Now she was on her feet, going to the bedroom bureau.

"If you don't believe me, look at the other notes I've written. I keep them all right here in my dresser. They don't mean a thing. Not a thing!"

Alison Kale yanked open the top drawer of the antique dresser. Then she suddenly went white as a sheet and let out a piercing scream!

There, perched on top of her lingerie, was Sarah Amberly's jewelry box.

Chapter

Nine

I HAVE NO idea how this got here!" Alison Kale was close to being hysterical now. "I swear, I didn't take this from Sarah's room. I would never do that. I wasn't jealous of my sister, no matter how wealthy she was. Money means nothing to me!"

Nancy couldn't help but believe the woman. Still, the jewelry box was in Alison's shaking hands. If *she* didn't put it in her drawer, who did? And why?

Nancy looked at the frightened woman and quickly sized things up. Recently, Alison had had a furious fight with Sarah, and before that, she'd written notes saying "Kill—Kill—Kill." And now the missing jewelry box was found in her drawer. This makes her look guilty, Nancy realized.

Alison Kale must also have been thinking the same thing, because the color drained from her face. "They'll think I killed Sarah. Then what'll I do? With Sarah dead, I have no one to turn to! My nephew thinks only of himself! And Pieter van Druten has always hated me. Who can I turn to now?"

Tears of panic were welling up in Alison's eyes, and she turned to Nancy, desperate. *"You!* You've got to help me. For Sarah's sake—take this!"

Alison thrust the jewelry box into Nancy's hands and ranted on. "Take this and get rid of it! I don't care what you do with it—just get it out of here!"

Nancy held the box gingerly in her hands, wondering what Joe Ritter would say if he walked into the room just then. As much as Nancy pitied Sarah's sister, there was little she could do to help her.

Holding the box out, Nancy shook her head. "I'm sorry, Miss Kale. I really ca—"

But she never had a chance to finish her sentence. Suddenly, at the front door, she heard a movement. Was someone eavesdropping on them?

"I'll be right back." Tossing the box lightly

onto the bed, Nancy fled from the room and out the front door. In the hallway a figure turned a corner. Nancy followed, but she couldn't see who the listener had been, or whether it was a man or a woman. One thing Nancy was sure of—it wasn't Maximilian. He was much shorter than this person.

Then Nancy saw a door to a stairwell close, and she heard footsteps hurrying down. Quickly she slipped into the same stairway. A few stories down, she heard another door open. The eavesdropper was getting away!

Nancy took the steps two at a time and ran out into another hallway until she saw another door slowly closing. She pulled that door open and found herself inside yet another stairway. She propelled herself down the stairs, pushing off against the banister.

On the ground floor she opened a door and was in a banquet-hall kitchen. All around her were waiters, waitresses, busboys, and cooks. In the midst of their activity, they glanced up at Nancy with uncomprehending looks. Nancy smiled awkwardly.

"Excuse me," she muttered, backing out of the great kitchen. Defeated, she made her way to the main bank of elevators and pressed *Penthouse*. Whoever had overheard her conversation with Alison knew about the jewels, thought Nancy, and might even think Nancy had them now. And whoever it was, the person was probably dangerous. Was it Jack Kale? Or Pieter van Druten? Or maybe even Madame Rosa?

She had chased him—or her—off for now, certainly, and getting out of the elevator, she suddenly felt hungry. She realized that she and her father hadn't had breakfast yet. Ah, well, thought Nancy, a little brunch at the Palm Court should fix that. Carson would be awake by now and ready to go. And the sooner the better.

Inside the suite, she called, "Dad? You up yet?"

A sleepy voice answered her from the master bedroom. "I'll be out in a minute, Nancy. Are you as hungry as I am?"

"I ought to be!" answered Nancy, with a glance at her watch. "Do you realize it's ten-thirty?"

"You're kidding!" said Carson, surprised. "I certainly got my beauty sleep, didn't I? I wouldn't know it by the way I feel, though," he added, stepping into the living room. He didn't look at all well rested. "Shall we go?" he asked, offering her his arm and yawning sleepily.

"Oh, just one minute, Dad, okay? I was chatting with Miss Kale, and I sort of left in midconversation."

Nancy could read the disapproval all over her father's face. "I knew you'd be trying to solve this case, Nancy," he said, "but I didn't think you'd be sniffing around before I even woke up! Be quick, will you? My stomach is sending urgent messages."

"Mine, too!" Nancy smiled, grateful that her dad was so understanding. "I'll meet you at the Palm Court."

Nancy ran to the Amberly suite. She wanted to settle the matter of hiding the jewels with Alison. The sooner the poor woman could be convinced to hand the box over to the police, the better. If she hadn't killed her sister—and something told Nancy she hadn't—then the best thing was to let the investigation take its course.

Hmmm, thought Nancy, if I were Alison Kale, would I trust a guy like Joe Ritter? He'd have a lot to say to the police, for sure.

She pushed open the door to Alison's room. "I lost him," she said as she entered. "Ran down about thirty flights of—"

Nancy suddenly realized that she was talking to an empty room. Alison was gone, and so was the jewelry box. And there, on the center of the bed, was another crumpled piece of paper.

"Kill—Kill—Kill—" Nancy read. It was the same piece of paper that had started this madness. But this time, stuck through it, pinning it to the mattress, was a foot-long butcher's knife!

Chapter
Ten

JUDGING BY THE way her father eyed her across their table in the Palm Court, Nancy could tell that he was not pleased. "A butcher's knife! Nancy, what next? You know, last night I kept having dreams about your being in solitary confinement."

Nancy stared down at her eggs.

"Even when you were three years old," he said, shaking his head, "you were searching for all the lost toys in the neighborhood. I should have known then . . ."

Only the tiniest glimmer in Carson's eyes convinced Nancy that he was joking.

"Sorry, Dad," Nancy mumbled, "but sometimes you've got to put yourself out there. You know how it is."

"Yes, I suppose I do," Carson replied with a sigh. "Anyway, I decided to go over and have a talk with Chief Harden at Interpol. Maybe he'll be able to keep that nasty house detective off your back."

Nancy reached down and opened her blue leather handbag. "Well, while you're there, Dad, I just happen to have a list of questions for the people at Interpol—a short list. If it's not too much trouble, that is." She handed her father a folded paper and tried to smile brightly. It might be the last straw for her father, but she had to take the chance.

Her father took the list, shaking his head. "You are too much, you know," he murmured, slipping the paper in his jacket pocket. "Heaven knows how you got this way."

"I guess I'm not your daughter for nothing," Nancy couldn't resist saying. As long as she could remember, people were telling her how much she and her dad were alike, and that it couldn't have been an accident that they were both interested in crime and the law.

For the first time all morning, Carson relaxed and smiled. "Well, I wouldn't trade you—not for all the *normal* daughters in the world."

Nancy smiled back, but her face clouded over

when she saw Joe Ritter striding into the Palm Court, heading for their table. "Uh-oh," she murmured.

"Well, if it isn't Mr. Drew and his lovely daughter, Nancy. Fancy meeting you here!" Joe Ritter blasted out.

"Fancy meeting *you* here is more like it," Carson muttered under his breath, his good mood broken by the sight of the house detective. "Would you care to join us?" he asked, hoping the man would pass them by.

Ritter had already helped himself to an extra chair and put it beside their table.

"Just thought you'd be interested in my latest discovery," the house detective said with a sickening smile. "I happen to know someone at the New York police lab, and apparently, Nancy's fingerprints are all over Sarah Amberly's pillbox."

Of course they were, Nancy thought. Hadn't she recently helped Sarah take her medication? But she said nothing.

And what about Sarah's jewelry box? Did Ritter know about that? If he weren't so smug, Nancy would have filled him in. But as it was, she decided, he'd probably turn it against her.

Still, she thought with a sigh, thank goodness she hadn't stashed the box for Alison.

"You know, the courts tend to be more lenient if you make a full confession," Ritter said.

From the look on her father's face, Nancy thought that at any minute there just might be more than one murder at the Plaza. "Pardon me, but I believe confessions are a *police* matter, Detective Ritter. As I understand it, your investigation here at the Plaza is in no way authorized by the state or any court of law. Now, please forgive us, but my daughter and I have personal business to discuss."

Nancy had to suppress a smile. Her dad was really something when he was angry. His years as a lawyer had trained him to be courteous at all times, but that just made the effect more devastating.

With a snort of disdain, Ritter stood up. "I was just going, anyway. In fact, I'm meeting with my contact in the police department in ten minutes. I just thought you'd be interested in knowing about the lab report," he said, backing away from the table. "Meanwhile, I advise you to stick around, Miss Drew."

"Good day, Mr. Ritter." Carson set his mouth in a straight line, but when he turned back to Nancy, he smiled. "Guess I'll just have to give our theater tickets to the Dutch police chief. I'm glad *someone* will get to the theater on this trip."

"Oh no! You mean she actually *died* while you were holding her?" Bess was horrified.

"Poor Nancy!" George Fayne was aghast, too.

"Poor *me?* What about Sarah Amberly? She was murdered!" Nancy flung herself down on the divan in her suite and looked over at her two stunned friends. "And guess who the house detective thinks did it?"

"Her sister? She is kind of nutsy, isn't she, Nan?" Bess was nibbling on a fingernail now.

"Well, yes. But she's not the kind of person who would commit murder. I don't think so, at least."

"Then who's the main suspect?" George wanted to know.

Nancy took a deep breath. "Ready for this? *I* am."

"Nancy, no!" Bess was on her feet, pacing. "That's terrible!"

"Terrible but true," Nancy stated. Though why she was taking it so calmly, she didn't know.

Just then, a knock interrupted the three girls. Nancy went to answer it. There in the doorway stood Jack Kale. He looked subdued, almost penitent, as he raised an eyebrow to take in Nancy and her friends.

Bess blinked about a dozen times. Jack's movie-star looks were obviously making a big impression on Nancy's pretty blond friend. George, too, seemed stunned by Jack's entrance. She instinctively looked away as if she were too dazzled to look at him.

"Hi. My name is Jack Kale. I don't believe

we've been properly introduced." He extended his hand to Nancy. "You're the murderess, I understand." He smiled gently and Nancy knew he was joking.

"Hi. I'm Nancy Drew, and these are my friends Bess Marvin and George Fayne, Mr. Kale."

"Oh, *Jack.* After all, we're likely to find ourselves behind bars together before too long." Again there was that devil-may-care laugh. But Nancy thought she could hear a catch in it this time, and there was a quick flash of sorrow in his deep blue eyes.

Then it was gone. He gave George and Bess a smile, and Nancy noted that George blushed deeply when he met her gaze.

"Has the house detective been on your case, too?" Nancy wanted to know.

"Very much so, I'm afraid. I came in at dawn, and he was waiting for me." Jack's eyes swept the room and he sighed. "Poor Aunt Sarah." There was silence for a moment.

"But," he went on, "I know there's nothing we can do for her now. Sooo . . ." Nancy felt the effort he was making to be cheerful. "Nice suite you've got here," he remarked.

He looked over at George for a reaction, and he got one—a crimson blush and a lowering of her head. Nancy was surprised—George wasn't usually the type to be instantly smitten, but then, Jack Kale was not a usual guy.

"Seriously, though," he continued, "you're obviously no more guilty than poor Aunt Alison. Or myself, for that matter. It's got to be Pieter, if you ask me. What do you think?"

"Well, he's pretty intense, I'll give him that," Nancy said soberly. "But he has an alibi. We ran into him at Trump Tower at the time of the murder."

"Oh. I see." Jack's forehead creased slightly. "I guess that's that, then. But that gives you an alibi, too. Have you told Ritter?"

"A hundred times." Nancy sighed. "But he's kind of—I don't know, *slow,* if you know what I mean."

"I know exactly what you mean." Jack nodded. "So I guess that leaves poor old Aunt Alison after all. Shocking. If I didn't know better, I'd say it was me. I seem to be the most likely villain."

"You certainly had enough reasons," Nancy said, a challenge in her voice.

Jack Kale ignored her, however, and turned instead to George. "It's George, right?" he went on. "Quite a name for a girl like you. If you'd like, George, we could have a little dinner together tonight. It may not be entirely appropriate, but I do have to eat, and it would help to cheer me up."

George was sitting bolt upright, stiff and uncomfortable. "Uh—" she stammered. "Nancy, could I talk with you for a minute—privately?"

"Sure thing," said Nancy, getting up. "Excuse us, will you?"

When George and Nancy had adjourned to Nancy's bedroom, George burst out in a loud whisper, "I can't go out with him! I can't even *look* at him, for goodness' sake!"

"What's the matter? Don't you like him?" Nancy asked.

"Nancy! Of course I like him! Those eyes, that face—what's not to like? Other than the fact that he might be a murderer, of course."

"Of course," agreed Nancy. "On the other hand, maybe you could find out a thing or two about him—as a favor to an old friend?"

"Well, if you really need me to," said George, breaking into a grin. "I guess I could suffer through an evening with the handsomest guy in the universe."

"Good. It's settled. I'll count on you to take good notes. There'll be a quiz in the morning."

George laughed. "You owe me one after this, Nan!" she said, with a wag of her finger.

"Don't worry, Fayne," Nancy assured her. "I'll think of something terrific I can do with you—besides setting you up with a gorgeous guy, that is."

"A guy who might just be a killer? Thanks for the favor," George said wryly.

"Somehow you seem more pleased than scared," said Nancy with a little smile. "I have faith in you, George." She patted her friend on the back. "You can handle it."

Back in the suite, Nancy and Bess talked and tried to ignore the hushed tones of Jack and George making plans at the door. When Nancy glanced at them from the corner of her eye, she noticed that George wasn't the only one who looked smitten; Jack Kale was practically gaga by the time he said his goodbyes. He even made George burst into giggles by taking her hand and kissing it.

"Till tonight," he said with a wink as he left.

George closed the door behind him, then collapsed against it with a deep sigh. "He's fantastic," she said dreamily. "Utterly and completely fantastic."

Bess rolled her eyes and smiled. Then her face turned serious. "Come on, Nancy—who did it?"

"Take it easy, Bess, it's too soon to know. There's Jack, Pieter, Alison—even Madame Rosa might be the culprit, or Maximilian, the waiter—something's up with him."

"Nancy, I bet it's Alison," Bess piped up. "Why else would she have run away? Maybe she stole the jewels and killed her sister—then, when you discovered the jewelry box, she had to run!"

"Maybe . . ." Nancy pursed her lips, unimpressed.

91

As for George, she had other things on her mind. "Did you notice his eyelashes? They have to be an inch long—and those eyes are pure amethyst. . . ."

But George's poetic rhapsodies were lost on Nancy. She was busy thinking about Alison Kale. She remembered Sarah saying not to blame Alison for whatever might happen. Did Sarah Amberly know that her sister might be dangerous? Or did she sense that someone else might want her to look that way?

"Where?" Nancy asked earnestly, thinking out loud. "Where did Alison go? Was she kidnapped? Has she been killed? Or is she in hiding? Right now, Alison Kale is the key to this mystery. Without her, we're as much in the dark as good old Joe Ritter."

"Nancy," Bess interjected, "in case you forgot, this is a big city. She could be anywhere! Where are we supposed to start looking for her?"

"Well," Nancy said thoughtfully, "why not at the beginning? In her bedroom, that is? Maybe she left some clue to her whereabouts."

Once again the three friends made their way silently to the Amberly suite and opened the door, which was unlocked.

"Oh, boy—this place is beginning to really scare me," muttered Bess as they made their way to Alison Kale's room and slowly pushed the door open.

Instantly, they froze in their tracks. There, sitting calmly on the bed, pointing a small silver pistol at them, was Pieter van Druten.

"Wait!" screamed Nancy. "Don't shoot!"

But it was too late. With a cruel smile on his lips, Pieter pulled the trigger.

Chapter

Eleven

Bang—YOU'RE DEAD!"

A small flame emerged from the hammerlock of the pistol. Pieter used it to light his cigar. "Fooled you, didn't I?" he said. "That will teach you to come barging into other people's rooms uninvited."

A cigarette lighter! The girls all nearly collapsed in relief. Bess giggled nervously, but Nancy and George were not amused in the least. "I notice you're in someone else's room yourself, Mr. van Druten," she pointed out.

"Ah, brilliant! You're a very observant young lady, Miss Drew," he said, complimenting her.

"I'm sure that's one of the things Sarah found so attractive about you." He blew a smoke ring in her direction. Coughing, Nancy waved her hand to disperse the noxious cloud.

"Of course," he continued, turning the cigar over in his fingers and regarding it lovingly, "the lady whose room we're all sitting in isn't here. Nor is she anywhere to be found. You, of course, Miss Drew, with your keen powers of observation, will have already noticed that fact."

Nancy nodded slowly, waiting for him to say more. Pieter van Druten obviously had a lot on his mind, and if she let him, Nancy was sure he would go on.

"Won't you have a seat—you and your charming young companions?" He gestured around the room at several chairs and a divan. Nancy, George, and Bess took seats, feeling rather uncomfortable and put off by Pieter's condescending tone.

"My, my—Sarah would have been so happy to see us all here together," he said, smirking a bit. "How I wish she could have been here. . . ." He carefully flicked the ash from his cigar into a marble ashtray at his elbow.

"Unfortunately, Sarah was simply not careful enough. She allowed her family to take advantage of her constantly—and *this* is how they have repaid her."

"Just what are you implying?" Nancy asked.

"Her nephew Jack has been robbing her blind

ever since her husband passed away," he said, watching the plume of blue smoke trailing up toward the ceiling. "And her sister—well, I told Sarah a thousand times to have her put away, for safety's sake, but she refused to listen, poor trusting soul. And look how she's been repaid."

"You're saying Alison Kale is responsible for Sarah Amberly's death? That's a pretty heavy charge." Nancy watched Pieter's face carefully. He shook his head lightly and sighed deeply.

"Well, you must agree, the woman is mad, completely mad. Did you know she was committed for several months when she attempted to take her own life a few years ago? She's totally irrational and she never could adjust to the fact that Sarah was out of her league in every way."

Nancy frowned. The one thing Alison Kale had *not* seemed was jealous. Shy, yes—even neurotic —but jealousy just hadn't seemed to enter into her relationship with her sister.

"They were born poor, you know," Pieter van Druten continued. "Dirt poor. Sarah was able to transcend the circumstances of her birth, but Alison was not. It's that simple.

"In fact, I informed Detective Ritter of all this not an hour ago. Someone had to let the poor man know of her disappearance. The entire police force is out there searching for her right now, their butterfly nets in hand, I suppose." With that, Pieter chuckled.

Nancy caught George's eye, and she could tell George was thinking the same thing she was: for a man who'd just lost his fiancée, Pieter van Druten seemed remarkably collected.

Nancy wondered if she should speak her mind in front of Pieter. Giving him the benefit of her thinking was like baiting a barracuda, she knew. On the other hand, she wanted to hear what else he had to say. There was something about him. . . .

"I think you're wrong," said Nancy. "This crime was too calculated for a person as unstable as Alison. She could never have planned it, much less carried it out."

Pieter van Druten threw Nancy a dazzling smile and stubbed out his cigar. "Brilliant, truly brilliant, Miss Drew. And that is where Jack Kale comes in. Between the two of them, they had one brain, and with that little brain they were able to plan and execute poor Sarah's demise."

Nancy saw George shiver when she heard that. That night, she and Jack would be off on their date together—alone.

"I don't understand," said Nancy, hoping Pieter would explain.

He did. "You see, Miss Drew, Sarah and I were to be married. If that happened, both Alison and Jack stood to lose millions. On their own, they are penniless, yet they've grown used to living the life of wealthy people through Sarah's generosity.

I myself"—again he laughed his cruel little laugh—"I am not so generous. They would have both been out on their ears and they knew it."

"Hmmm." Nancy considered Pieter's hypothesis. It certainly sounded logical. And then there was the little matter of the jewels. She wondered if Pieter knew Alison had them. If he did, then he'd been the one eavesdropping on them. He may have even planted them in Alison's dresser.

"Then why steal the jewels?" she asked him. "With Sarah out of the way, wouldn't they have come to Alison and Jack in the end?"

Pieter considered this for a long moment. "Who knows?" he answered. "The working of irrational minds is hard to comprehend."

"You seem to do all right," Nancy remarked.

"Surely, Miss Drew, you are not suggesting that *I* took the jewels?" He laughed uproariously. "You may not be aware, but I am the owner of a rather large diamond mine of my own, back home. Money is of no interest to me, my dears. It was Sarah I was after. I loved her. I'm sure you shared my regard for her—her special qualities—"

Nancy couldn't help but wonder what Sarah had seen in Pieter van Druten. True, he was handsome and debonair, but Sarah Amberly wasn't the type to go for surface appeal. She was deeper than that. And van Druten was so calculating, so unlikable—had Sarah truly intended to marry a man like him?

It really was too bad, she thought. Pieter would make such a perfect murderer. If only he had had a motive. And if only he hadn't had such an ironclad alibi. But Nancy had seen him with her very own eyes in Trump Tower at the time of the murder.

Just then, they heard shouting outside, followed by a woman's screams. "Get your filthy hands off me!" she cried out at the top of her lungs.

"I believe our fugitive has been found," said Pieter as Joe Ritter and several policemen entered with Alison Kale in tow. She was kicking and shouting. In Felske's hands was the missing jewelry box.

"Aha!" said Pieter, delighted. "All the loose ends seem to be falling into place."

"We found her, Mr. van Druten," Detective Ritter bragged. "She was trying to hide the box up on the roof." Then he turned to Nancy. "But you're not off the hook yet, missy," he said, pointing his finger at her. "I'm arresting this lady for robbery, but the murder charge is still open and up for grabs, understand?"

Nancy was about to explode. She had taken enough from Joe Ritter, and she was going to tell him so in no uncertain terms.

But she never got the chance. Because just at that moment, Felske tripped over the leg of a table, sending the jewelry box flying end over end. It popped open as it landed, spilling a rainbow of gems all over the marble floor in front of the fireplace.

"Holy smokes!" said Ritter, looking down at his feet. He stopped to pick up a handful of glittering fragments. The diamonds, rubies, and emeralds had smashed into a thousand pieces.

Ritter looked around the room, flabbergasted. "These jewels are fakes—every last one of them!"

Chapter

Twelve

A CHARGED SILENCE filled the room. It was broken only by Alison's scream.

"I didn't kill her, I swear it! Why doesn't anyone believe me? Why? Sarah—Sarah, you've got to tell them, please, I didn't kill you! I didn't steal your jewels!"

The poor woman was suddenly reduced to a babbling bundle of terrified humanity. The hotel doctor, who had entered right behind the security men, was on her in a moment, administering a sedative by hypodermic. And after a few moments, Alison collapsed in a heap on the floor.

Felske and one of the policeman carried her out of the room.

"Okay, everybody," Ritter barked. "I want you to get back to your rooms and stay there till you're interviewed by the police. And where's the nephew—that's what I want to know!"

"Excuse me," said Bess, in as respectful a tone as she could manage. "You're not including us in that order, are you? We're not even staying at the Plaza."

As she was speaking, Ritter took Bess in from top to toe, and he looked very impressed. "No, no, you and your friend here," he said, indicating George, "are free to go. But *you*"—now he pointed to Nancy—"stay here."

George looked at Nancy as if to say, "This guy is too much," and for a second, Nancy almost felt sorry for him—he seemed so hopelessly foolish.

"Well, Nancy, we'd better go," George said. "My date tonight, remember? I've got to decide what to wear! Wish me luck."

"That's enough chitchat!" Ritter yelled.

Nancy shot Ritter a withering look before turning to her dark-haired friend. "I do wish you luck, George. And be careful!"

"Bye, Nancy," called Bess. "We'll call you later, okay?"

"Great," Nancy answered, while the detective rolled his eyes impatiently. "I'm having dinner right here in the hotel, I guess. I hope my dad will be with me."

After her two friends left, Nancy watched the policemen gather up the shattered "jewels." They put the fragments they collected into plastic bags for lab analysis. Finally, she spoke up. "Mr. Ritter, if you don't need me—"

"What, are you still here?" said Ritter.

"Not anymore," Nancy replied, making her way out of the room.

Back in her own suite, Nancy opened the door on a silent living room. On the coffee table was a note from Carson: "Nancy, I'm held up at Interpol. Order dinner without me, but I should be able to join you for dessert."

So much for their dinner together. Another lost cause.

Feeling unsettled, Nancy slid open the huge louvered doors of her closet and looked at her clothes. The new peach outfit was just sitting there. She had wanted to wear it to the Broadway show. . . . Well, she'd wear it that night, no matter what. Even if the weekend was falling apart, she still wanted to look good. Maybe she'd call Bess, and the two of them could go to the Oak Room by themselves.

A low rumbling filled the room, and Nancy realized it was her stomach. No wonder—she had missed lunch, and dinnertime was still several hours away. Thank goodness for room service.

"Please send a small fruit and cheese board to my suite, with a club soda, please," Nancy said into the phone. Hanging up, she walked over to the triple window facing Fifth Avenue and tried to clear her mind. But it was pretty hard to ignore the fact that she was practically under house arrest at the Plaza Hotel. What a weekend!

She hadn't meant to get herself into such an awful mess, of course. And really, her own problems were nothing compared to the other things that had happened—like murder. Nancy had to get to the bottom of it and see that the murderer was put away where he, or she, couldn't hurt anyone else. Leaving Sarah's murder in the hands of the authorities would, in this case, be like walking away from the scene of an accident. She might be the only one who could figure out what had really happened.

Maximilian arrived with a tray containing the fruit and cheese board and a bottle of club soda.

"Hello, again, miss," he greeted her.

"Hello, Maximilian," she replied wearily.

The little waiter left the tray on the table in front of her and made for the door. He did not leave, however. Instead, he turned and said, "Perhaps, miss, you will permit me to give you a little piece of advice?"

Nancy looked up at him in stark surprise. "Well, what is it?" she asked, annoyed and curious at the same time.

"This matter of the Amberlys—miss, I urge you, for your own safety, to stay away from it. It is not something for a nice young girl like you.

You, you should be at the parties, the discos, with the young boys, having a good time. Not here, in this nest of snakes and evil things." He moved in close to her, his eyes piercing.

"Please, miss, it will end badly for you. Please . . ."

Nancy took a deep breath. "I appreciate your concern, Maximilian, but you see, I liked Sarah Amberly. And I don't think the person who murdered her should walk away."

Maximilian's face darkened. "That old witch! You liked her? Ha! She was as bad as all the rest of them. Forget her, I tell you! Forget her, before it is too late! You do not understand these things, these matters are deadly, miss—"

"I beg your pardon," Nancy interrupted him, "but I know what I'm doing. This isn't the first time I've been involved with—well, with murder. And I don't intend to let the criminal get away with it."

"So." Maximilian nodded, tight-lipped, "You will not listen. You fancy yourself a detective. You cannot let the murderer get away with it, you say. Allow me to tell you, miss—in this world, everyone gets away with whatever he can. We all do whatever it takes to get by, understand?"

His voice was hoarse now, the muscles of his face twitching with rage. "You rich people, you think everything is easy! You never get your hands dirty, yet you live like kings and turn your noses up at the rest of us. Well, allow me to tell you, *I* have come a long, long way to get where I am now. See?"

He held out his hands to her, palms upward. "See these hands? Maybe you do not see the dirt on them, but it is there, inside. . . . I know what it is, miss, to want things, and to do anything to get them."

Spinning on his heel, he strode to the door. Then, standing in the doorway, he turned and said, "I have warned you, miss. Stay out of this matter. I will not warn you again." And then he was gone.

"Wow! What do you think he meant?" Bess's eyes widened with surprise as Nancy told her about Maximilian's warning.

The two girls were sitting at a table in the Oak Room, pretending to read their menus, but all the while they kept sneaking glances in the waiter's direction.

Maximilian studiously ignored them as he went about serving his tables on the other side of the Oak Room.

"I don't know what he meant," Nancy admitted. "And I guess I never will know. But he sure is creepy, isn't he?"

"Nancy! Wait a minute. I just got an idea!" Bess whispered excitedly. "Maybe *he* did it! He always brought her tea, right?"

"Maximilian? Murder Sarah? I don't know."

Nancy sighed, shaking her head. "I mean, I guess anything is possible——"

"Oh no!" Bess's attention was caught by a movement at the front of the restaurant. "Don't look now, but here comes trouble."

Nancy did look, and what she saw was Joe Ritter striding toward their table, an angry scowl on his face.

"I suppose you think you're a real big shot," he hissed as he pulled up a chair and sat down without being invited. "Your precious father seems to have turned some screws on high. I just got a call telling me to go easy on you or take early retirement."

Nancy and Bess looked at each other, and neither one of them could suppress a giggle of satisfaction. Good old Carson to the rescue!

"Oh? You find that amusing? Well, don't get the idea you're permanently off the hook," Ritter warned Nancy. "A man in my position has to follow his instincts. My instincts tell me you're hiding something, and I intend to find out what it is." His jaw was set determinedly.

The three of them sat in stony silence for all of thirty seconds, none of them knowing what to say.

Finally, Ritter grabbed a menu and said, with a wink at Bess, "So, what are you having?"

The girls' jaws dropped open. Was he actually going to invite himself to dinner, after being so nasty not half a minute before?

107

"As for you," he said, returning to Nancy, "I know you know more than you're telling, so why don't you spill the beans right here and now? I'll pick up the tab. Deal?"

Nancy just couldn't look Bess in the eyes. If she did, she'd end up giggling again! Obviously, bumbling Joe Ritter was a desperate man, and he was asking for their help in his own crude way. Well, she wasn't going to tell him *everything,* but Nancy supposed it couldn't hurt to share some of her thoughts with the befuddled detective.

"Honestly, what I know is very simple, and it's all public information. A woman dies from an overdose of her own medicine, and apparently her jewelry box is taken at the same time. Now, why was she murdered? Well, not for her jewels. For one thing, they were fakes. But more important, those jewels were used to implicate her sister. Right after the murder they're planted in Alison's bureau drawer where anyone could find them."

Ritter's brow was screwed up in concentration as he tried to follow Nancy. "Wait a minute," he interjected. "What if Alison didn't know the jewels were fakes? Maybe she didn't open the box after the murder because she was planning to run away with it."

Nancy sighed and absentmindedly began to line up the silverware in front of her. As a sleuth, Joe Ritter was truly hopeless. "No, no. A confused person like Alison would never be able to carry through with such a cool plan—not in my opinion, at least. Yes, the person who murdered Sarah Amberly knew her habits, knew that she took her medicine with her tea in the evening, and yes, they knew just how potent that medicine really was. But Alison Kale plan a murder? No way. She's too confused and hysterical. The only way she could ever hurt anyone would be in an unplanned outburst of anger, nothing calculated."

"How do you know she just didn't *force* the medicine on the old lady out of anger?" Ritter demanded.

"Anyone who ever saw the two of them together could answer that question. Alison was angry at Sarah, all right, but she was also afraid of her. She let Sarah lead her. But honestly, the bottom line is they loved each other."

"Well, *somebody* did it." Ritter was shaking his head in frustration. Suddenly Nancy thought back to the very first time she saw Sarah Amberly walking down the hall. "My medicine is always running low— Why can't one of you look after it. . . ."

Of course! Even back then, someone could have been putting tablets aside. Nancy was just about to share that memory when she noticed Maximilian across the room, standing on tiptoe, gesturing to someone. Obviously, he was trying to catch that person's attention—trying hard, to judge from the way he was waving. But who was he waving to? And now he was walking off toward that someone.

"Would you two excuse me, please? I've got to go to the ladies' room."

Throwing down her napkin, Nancy rose and threaded her way between the tables in the direction the waiter had taken. Out of the restaurant, around the corner of the hallway, and—where?

Ah, there was his white towel on the floor. It must have fallen out of his uniform pocket. Nancy sped down the corridor, just in time to see a pneumatic door swing shut. She hurried through it, ignoring the sign that said Employees Only, and found herself at the top of a staircase.

Nancy flew down the stairs, pausing only when she reached a corridor that was lit by bare bulbs. The floor was concrete, painted gray. No luxury here. Off in the distance, Nancy heard the hum of immense motors, and something else—the click of footsteps!

Now she could hear the footsteps quickening to a run, and as she followed, she could also hear the roar of motors getting louder. This had to be the loading dock where trash was piled into the hotel's compactor and from there taken by trucks to the city dump.

Nancy halted and listened for the footsteps. They had stopped. After a moment, she proceeded again, slowly, taking each step lightly and listening hard for any telltale sound.

Suddenly she felt strong hands grip her from behind. And the next thing she knew she was hurtling headfirst down a chute that was in the wall opposite her.

She landed with a thud, in a dark place with a vaguely disgusting smell. It was dark down there, only a square of light at the end of the sort of tunnel she was in. The floor was soft, rubbery. Nancy wondered where she was.

But when the floor started moving to the tune of a whirring motor, Nancy knew. She was on a conveyor belt. And the square of light, now growing larger, was the mouth of the compactor!

Rising unsteadily to her feet, Nancy started to inch back to where she had landed. Just then, however, a chute opened somewhere above her, and a huge pile of trash landed smack on top of her, sending her sprawling to the floor. Among the papers Nancy noticed some orange rinds, several loaves of stale bread, and some coffee grounds.

Nancy flailed about anxiously, trying in vain to dig herself out and get to her feet again. But it was impossible. Every passing second brought her closer to the great mouth of the compactor. In no time at all she'd be reduced to a cube the size of a shoe box!

Chapter

Thirteen

NANCY MOVED HER hands around frantically, desperately feeling for some way to escape the huge jaws of the compactor. They were coming closer and closer every moment!

Brushing coffee grounds out of her eyes, she tried to claw her way backward, but it was no use. Just a few feet ahead, the two-ton mechanical monster was thudding down and she was headed straight for it.

But then, just as she was about to have the life squashed out of her, there was a shower of sparks and the giant motor came to a grinding halt. All at once there was total silence and total darkness.

Even the dim square of light behind Nancy had disappeared.

It must be a power outage, Nancy thought. Swallowing hard, she stood up. Her shoulder bumped painfully against a wall of the stalled compactor.

Nancy knew that hotels like the Plaza had emergency lighting systems that turned on automatically in cases like this. That meant the compactor would shortly be working again. She had, at the most, a minute to save herself.

Twisting out of the compactor's way, she felt behind her—more trash. She scrambled madly through the enormous pile ahead of her until she reached the chute she had come down.

Nancy tried to pull herself up by grabbing the walls of the chute, but they were too slick. At last she managed to locate a chink in one wall. It was just big enough to accommodate her right hand. She gripped it and pulled with all her might. Thank goodness, it worked. She was able to take her first steps back up the chute.

The second her feet left the conveyor belt, the emergency power switched on, and the belt kicked into motion again with a whirring noise. Behind her, Nancy heard the compactor come down with a sickening crunch. That could have been me, she thought, her stomach tightening.

Pulling her way up for what seemed like an eternity, she finally came to the top of the chute and, with a final thrust, threw herself over the top and landed on the cold floor of the underground hallway.

The emergency lighting left a lot to be desired. It cast deep shadows, and Nancy had to feel her way along the corridor until she heard hushed voices and saw a faint glimmer of light at the end of the catacombs.

Through the window of the pneumatic door, Nancy could see the eerily lit lobby. She pushed the door open and began walking back toward the Oak Room.

All around her, the hotel staff was busily tending to their patrons' comfort, reassuring them that everything was all right.

"I was reading my paper when the lights went out! What happened?" asked a portly gentleman in a pin-striped suit.

"Our apologies, sir. There seems to have been some sort of power outage. Our maintenance staff is attending to it now, and we should have full power restored momentarily," explained one of the staff.

The portly man lifted his head when Nancy walked by. "Good Lord!" he exclaimed quietly.

"Heavens!" muttered a woman, making a face at Nancy as she passed. But Nancy barely noticed. Her mind was in a whir. Someone had pushed her right to the brink of a horrible death, and only luck had saved her.

Pushing the carved oak doors open, Nancy sighed with relief. There was Bess, still seated with Detective Ritter, just as Nancy had left them not long before.

Hurrying toward her friend, she thought she heard sniffing sounds behind her. Sorry, folks, she felt like saying, but there was no sense bringing any more attention to herself. The pungent odor she gave off was noticeable enough.

So much for my new outfit, she thought, looking down at the stained jacket and skirt. Trying hard to maintain her dignity, she brushed some coffee grounds from her sleeve and made her way back to the table.

To Nancy's surprise, Ritter was leaning in close to Bess, obviously flirting. For her part, Bess seemed super uncomfortable but was obviously trying her best not to offend the lieutenant.

"Ahem," said Nancy. The two of them jumped when they heard her voice.

"Nancy!" cried Bess when she saw her friend. "What happened to you?"

Nancy glanced over at Ritter, who was looking her up and down in total shock. No way was she going to give him the pleasure of telling him what had really happened. Things were embarrassing enough as it was.

"Never mind about me," she said quickly.

"There's something we have to check out. Can you take us to the power grid?"

The detective hadn't quite recovered from the sight of the disarrayed Nancy. "Why do you want to get involved with a power outage?" he demanded to know. "The hotel people and Con Edison can take care of it without your help."

"Please!" she insisted. "I don't think we should waste any time."

Slowly Ritter rose from his chair, glowering at Nancy. "You're a weirdo, you know it?" he said, shaking his head. "All right, come on, I'll see what I can do."

Ritter led them down into the catacombs where Nancy had so recently had her brush with death. "The grid must be around here somewhere," he muttered.

"Nancy," Bess whispered as they went, "are you okay?"

"Yes, but you'll never believe what just happened," Nancy replied. Then, turning her attention back to their little expedition, she asked Ritter, "Are you sure you know the way?"

"Don't worry," he replied huffily, "I was a Boy Scout once." But he seemed completely confused by the maze of hallways they were in.

Finally they came to a door with a sign that read DANGER—EXTREMELY HIGH VOLT-

AGE. "This must be the place," said Ritter, pushing on the door.

As the door swung open, all three of them gasped in horror. There, attached to the grid, was Maximilian the waiter.

His eyes were wide open in surprise, but Maximilian saw nothing. He was dead.

Chapter

Fourteen

ALL RIGHT! STEP back! Don't touch a thing! I don't want any evidence tampered with!" Joe Ritter was in his element. He ordered Nancy and Bess back from the scene of Maximilian's death and whipped a small black walkie-talkie from his pocket.

"Okay, fellas—can you hear me? We got a little mess here at the Plaza. A little accident up here on the main power grid. A guy's been electrocuted. Send me some support right away."

"Oh, I'll never fall asleep tonight. Not with that in my brain." Bess turned away and shut her eyes tightly.

Nancy slipped an arm around her friend's shoulders. "I'm sorry you had to see this, Bess. I should have suspected—" She tried to comfort her.

Within minutes the place was swarming with police photographers and fingerprinters. Nancy and Bess stood around watching the professionals at work for a while. Then they decided to go back up to Nancy's suite so Nancy could change her clothes.

Later, up in the suite, a kind of grim mood overcame them. It was hard to shake the memory of Maximilian's death. And even worse for Nancy was knowing that his murderer was still out there.

"Maximilian knew too much, I'm sure of it," Nancy murmured. She was curled up on the divan, running her fingers through her freshly washed hair, trying to sort everything out.

Bess leaned on an elbow. "But *what* did he know, Nancy?"

A triple knock on the door told them George was there.

Bess ran to the door and flung it open. There was George, her back to the room. Out in the hall behind her, Jack Kale was throwing her a wave. "I don't suppose you'd like to do this again, would you?" he was saying.

"Actually, I would." George's knees practically buckled as she spoke.

"Maybe next time I can see you in River

Heights," he said with a little laugh. "Well, I guess I should say good night."

"Till next time," replied George with a shy smile. "Night, Jack—"

Bess felt she might as well be invisible. George watched Jack walk back to his suite as if in slow motion. Finally, when he was out of sight, George headed into the room. She seemed blissfully unaware—of her friends, the open door, her handbag, her jacket. . . . She sighed over and over again with happiness.

"So?" Bess giggled, her spirits finally lightening after the grisly discovery they'd made at dinner.

George looked around, as if waking up and noticing where she was for the first time. "Oh, Bess, Nancy . . ." she murmured. "Hi."

Nancy and Bess shot each other amused looks. It wasn't often that their poised friend acted so out of it.

"Sooooo . . ." Nancy tried this time.

"Oh—" replied George. "You want to know about Jack? He's wonderful. So—charming, so—" Her eyes lit up at the very thought of Jack Kale.

"So handsome?" Bess finished for her.

"Yes, and sweet, too. Very sweet. Incredibly sweet, in fact." George sat in a club chair with a rapturous smile plastered on her face.

"I take it he didn't try to murder you?" Nancy asked with an amused smile.

"Oh, no. Nancy, it *can't* be him. He's just too wonderful. He took me to an incredible place for dinner and then to this gambling parlor in the East Eighties."

Bess's eyes grew big. "Gambling's illegal."

"Oh, Bess, I know that! Anyway, he dropped five thousand dollars or so, but he said he could afford it."

Nancy's eyebrows went up. Jack Kale's only real connection to wealth was his aunt. Five thousand dollars was a lot of money to blow in one night!

After a few moments George seemed to be waking from the trance she was in. The smile was still there, but there was also a glimmer of the old level-headed George coming through what she was saying.

"He's not really *bad*. At least, I don't think so. But he does have a problem—he is messed up about money, you know? He takes big chances and then he panics. That's what I saw tonight, anyway."

"What do you mean, he panics?" Nancy asked.

George's eyes flickered with disappointment. "He admitted stealing the ruby. He said he was only going to use it as collateral for a loan, and he swore he was going to give it back. But honestly, Nancy, he really loved Sarah. He was awfully grateful that she and Joshua raised him. Imagine how hard it is to be an orphan."

It was plain to see George was smitten, but her

121

instincts about people were always on the mark, Nancy knew. If George Fayne thought Jack Kale was okay, Nancy had to believe it. That is, unless George had completely flipped.

Just to make sure, Nancy put it to her directly. "George, be honest, have you lost your mind over this guy?"

George looked up at her friend and considered the question carefully. "Well, maybe a little, Nancy. I mean, I'd never want to get involved with someone who gambled. And I really don't approve of him taking the ring—but I swear, Jack Kale would never hurt a fly. He's not the type."

That sounded more like George.

"So it *was* Jack who took the ring. I wonder if he took the jewelry box, too." Nancy was thinking out loud now.

"Oh, no. I forgot to tell you. Jack thought that whole theft was a real hoot. He always knew all the jewels in that box were fakes. Whenever they stayed at the Plaza, Sarah kept her good stuff in the hotel safe—except for the ruby, of course."

"Well, if we rule out Jack Kale . . ." Nancy was on her feet, pacing. Then she fell silent and looked up at the ceiling.

Bess looked up, too, and saw nothing there but carved plaster roses. "So, Nancy, who did it?" she wanted to know.

Nancy bit her lip and answered slowly. "Knowing who did it doesn't do much good unless you can prove it, Bess. And there's only one way I can do that."

"And that one way is?" asked George.

"I need some stationery." Moving to the rosewood desk, Nancy pulled out three sheets of embossed Plaza Hotel notepaper.

"Here goes," she murmured, scribbling furiously.

Bess and George watched as she wrote a message on each sheet of paper. She tucked each sheet into a separate envelope, sealed them, and stood up.

"Come on, guys," she said, heading for the door and making her way to the Amberly suite.

The suite was locked for once, but Nancy, taking her lock pick out of her pocket, promptly sprang the lock and walked in. Bess and George watched as she placed the envelopes one by one under Alison, Jack, and Pieter's doors.

That done, she motioned them back to her suite. "It's just a matter of time now. Soon the murderer will walk right up to our door," she announced confidently.

"Okay. I can't resist any longer. Out with it! What did you write?" Bess's blue eyes were sparkling with curiosity.

"Here's the message," answered Nancy. "I wrote: 'I know you killed her, and I can prove it. What's it worth to you? Meet me at my suite. I'll be waiting—*alone.*'"

"Ugh," muttered Bess. "Somehow the thought

of meeting a murderer face-to-face just doesn't thrill me." Nancy could tell that the picture of Maximilian was in her mind.

"Come on, let's get ready," said Nancy. Bess and George threw her confused looks, but Nancy moved straight ahead.

"Okay, George, you're the tallest. Here's a step stool to put by the door and a net to drop, courtesy of Prince Ururu of Rarotonga. He stayed in this suite before us, so if it smells of fish, it *should.*

"Bess, I have a starter's pistol for you. My dad was using it for a skit at the Interpol convention. When the door opens, aim it straight at the person's heart, and whatever you do, act like you mean business."

"You want me to shoot this thing?" Bess took the gun from Nancy as if it were molten lava.

"It's only a starter's pistol," said George from her position on the step stool next to the door.

"Don't shoot it, whatever you do!" Nancy advised. "Just *look* like you're *going* to shoot it at the first false move."

Shaking her blond waves, Bess took the pistol and focused on the door with a steely look. "The things I do for you, Nancy Drew!" she muttered. "I hope you appreciate me."

"You know I do," Nancy smiled sweetly, her rope ready.

The three friends stayed in their positions for

about ten minutes, the tension in the room palpable. Then, it happened.

With a creak, the doorknob turned, and the door slowly swung open.

Instantly the girls went into action. George's net came down over the head, Bess aimed straight for the heart, and Nancy swept her rope under the ankles, tripping up the unsuspecting visitor, who went down to the floor with a cry of outrage and a resounding thud.

"Hit the light, Bess!" Nancy cried excitedly. "We've got our killer!"

Bess did as she was told, while Nancy put a full-nelson hold on their prey. Blinking in the light, the three hunters got their first look at the murderously angry face of the man they had just caught—Carson Drew!

Chapter

Fifteen

WHAT IN THE name of . . . ?" Carson Drew tried to kick his way out of the dusty netting as the embarrassed girls freed him. "Is this your idea of a joke?"

George and Bess looked at each other, then at Nancy. They were all speechless. Carson shook his head.

"Awfully childish, if you ask me," he muttered, brushing the dust from his suit. Suddenly he stopped and looked hard at his daughter. "This isn't a joke, is it?" he asked, peering into her eyes.

"Dad, I'm sorry. I'll explain everything later.

Right now, I can't. I'm *this* close to solving the case." Nancy's palms almost touched.

Carson looked at her for a long moment, then nodded. "Just take care of yourself, will you?"

"I will," Nancy promised.

"And by the way, here's the information you wanted from Interpol." Carson drew an envelope from his inside jacket pocket and handed it to Nancy. She opened it and began reading with intense concentration.

"Hmmm," she murmured, nodding her head slowly.

"I hope it helps," said Carson, with more than a tinge of fatigue. "I had to sweat blood to get it. Interpol usually reserves case histories for registered members of police forces."

"Dad," said Nancy, looking up and tucking the papers back into the envelope, "I can't thank you enough. This is great, really. Now, I know this is a bit much to ask, but—"

"Hold it right there," said Carson, putting up a hand and shaking his head. "If you're going to ask me to go back and get you more information . . ."

"Just one or two more things, really, Dad," begged Nancy. "I'm so close, so close!"

Carson took a deep breath. "Sometimes I wish I had become a baker. That way if you got involved with my business—"

Nancy looked up from the table where she was

writing down her request for information.
"Dad," she said soberly, stopping his thought. "I
appreciate what you're doing for me."

"I know," said Carson. "Give me the request.
I'll see what I can do."

"Thanks, Dad," said Nancy, hugging him and
stuffing the paper in his suit pocket. "When
you're old and gray, I'll take good care of you, I
promise."

"Never mind that." Carson laughed, rising
tiredly to his feet. "Just promise me you'll make
our matinee Sunday. We've missed one show
already."

"I wouldn't miss this one if my life depended
on it," Nancy said, planting a quick kiss on her
father's cheek.

"Bye, girls," he said, going to the door. "I'm
going to see if I can wake anyone connected with
Interpol. Be careful. All right?"

"Promise," said Nancy, already planning her
next move.

The minute the door closed behind him, the
three girls took up their positions. Bess and
George had been in some pretty tight situations
with Nancy, so remaining still and quiet wasn't
so bad, except that it gave them time to consider
what a terrifying thing they were doing.

An hour went by, and still nothing had happened. The three friends began to grow uncom-

fortable and nervous in the darkness of the room. Only the shadows thrown by the city lights gave them any sense of where things were in the room.

Nancy couldn't help worrying. This was her last chance to catch her quarry. If the killer didn't rise to the bait, all her work would have been for nothing. Sarah Amberly's killer would get away, and Nancy would have to go back to River Heights empty-handed.

But time was running out. Nancy knew she couldn't ask George and Bess to hang around much longer. They were frightened, and they had good reason. If the murderer *did* show up, the odds were he'd be armed—and they knew it.

Bess kept sniffling and blowing her nose. The dust from the netting was getting to her. George was bearing up somewhat better, but Nancy knew that her friends' patience was wearing thin. This wasn't their idea of a good time in New York City.

To pass the time, Bess started to tell a ghost story. It was one she'd heard around the fire at camp, a long time ago. Then George told one, and then Nancy. By the time midnight rolled around, their nerves were jumping.

"What was that?" screamed Bess, when a window rattled in its casing. The others nearly leaped out of their skins. They were walking a razor's edge, and the tension was high.

"Nancy, come on." Bess sighed. "Can't we just

forget the whole thing? I mean, this is the Big Apple! There's one huge party going on down there, and we're missing all the fun!"

"Bess has a point, Nan," agreed George. "This doesn't exactly seem to be panning out. Can't we—"

Suddenly the girls fell deadly silent. A floorboard had creaked outside—someone was coming!

"I sure hope it isn't my dad again," whispered Nancy.

"What do you mean?" said George, her jaw tight with terror. "If it's not your dad, then—"

Their eyes fell to the doorknob as it started to turn. It clicked, and the door creaked slowly open.

Just then, just when they had the killer in their grasp, Bess leaned back and sneezed the biggest, noisiest "kerchoo" in world history.

As quickly as the door had opened, it shut again, and running footsteps sounded down the hall.

"Bess!" said George angrily. "How could you?"

"Never mind that!" said Nancy. "After him!"

Throwing down the net, the girls ran into the hall, making for the elevator bank. They got there just in time to see a raincoated figure duck into a closing elevator.

"He's heading for the lobby! Come on!" yelled Nancy. The girls ducked into the next elevator.

Bess pushed *L* about a hundred times. Nancy leaned against the wall of the car and gathered her strength as they headed down.

"I'm *so* glad I wore my running shoes," said George, looking down at her high-heeled pumps with a weak smile.

Nancy tried to smile back, but she was too tense. Her heart racing, she peered up at the elevator indicator making its way from the penthouse to the lobby. The antique brass markers seemed to crawl.

And when the doors opened on the seventh floor to admit a party of Japanese sightseers, her heart almost stopped. After what seemed an eternity, the three friends finally poured out of the elevator into the lobby, looking around for their quarry.

"We couldn't have missed him!" George said, more in hope than in confidence.

"But which way did he go?" asked Bess. "The Plaza exits let out on three different streets."

It was Nancy who noticed the swirl of khaki material in the glass revolving doors. "There!" she cried. Once outside, the three girls watched as the figure sprinted up to the hansom cab parked beside the curb on Fifty-ninth Street.

They saw him push aside the stunned carriage driver, who landed on the pavement. The figure in the raincoat hopped into the driver's seat, cracked the reins, and took off, heading into the park. The driver picked himself up and started

131

shouting and running after his cab in hopeless pursuit.

Nancy and her friends weaved through the careening traffic, waving their hands up over their heads and ignoring the red Don't Walk sign.

"Sorry!" yelled Bess at the irate drivers who blew their horns at them in a rhythmic city cacophony.

Another hansom cab was parked across the street. Its driver was standing on the curb, a cup of coffee in his hand, shocked that someone had stolen a cab.

"Cab!" called Nancy.

"Are you available?" asked Bess as they ran up to him.

The driver looked over, obviously trying to decide what to do. Should he follow the other cab or take this fare? "Sure, honey. Hop in." So saying, he turned to tell the chauffeur of a stretch limo what had happened.

Nancy watched the other horse-drawn cab disappear into Central Park. "Please, sir—we've got to hurry!" she cried.

"Just a minute, just a minute," he said.

"We don't *have* a minute!" George yelled, climbing into the driver's seat as Nancy and Bess clambered into the passenger seat.

"Hey! What are you girls doing?" screamed the driver.

Nancy turned back and shrugged. "Sorry, it's

an emergency!" With that, George cracked the reins and they were off.

The *clip-clop* of the horse's hooves turned to a fast gallop. Nancy and Bess had to hold tight to the edge of their seats to keep from falling. But George had done it—the other cab was in sight.

"Stop!" Nancy yelled at the top of her lungs as they pulled closer. "Stop!"

The intruder in the first cab turned to see how close they were, and in that moment George was able to gain on him, cutting the distance between the two carriages in half.

Around the scalloped curves of Central Park Drive they went, dodging angry motorists who swerved to avoid them. At Eighty-third Street, where the great gray bulk of the Metropolitan Museum loomed up out of the night, the girls' cab pulled up almost beside the lead carriage.

Thinking quickly, and acting even faster, Nancy climbed over a stunned Bess and opened the low door of the cab. "Wish me luck!" she shouted, before taking a flying leap.

"Nancy—*No!*" Bess cried out, too late. In horror, she watched as Nancy grabbed hold of the other cab just in time to avoid falling and being crunched under the rear wheels and those of the oncoming traffic.

Nancy climbed to the roof of the cab, unnoticed by its driver, who was intent on making his getaway.

133

Finally, with lightning speed, Nancy pounced, landing a karate chop to the base of the driver's skull. He slumped forward, letting the reins go limp.

Instantly, to stop him from falling, Nancy grabbed the unconscious driver with one hand and reached for the reins with the other. She pulled the horses to a halt at the side of the road.

Bess and George drew up just in front of them and ran to where Nancy was bent over the limp figure. They strained to see better as Nancy removed the oversize hat, revealing the face of Pieter van Druten!

Just then, the wail of a police siren split the night, and an officer came running, his gun drawn.

"What in the world is going on here?" he cried.

"Take us to the Plaza Hotel, officer," said Nancy, rising to her feet. "We've just caught a murderer!"

Chapter

Sixteen

"A<small>LL RIGHT</small>, M<small>ISS</small> Drew, now suppose you just start at the beginning and tell us what this is all about." Detective Ritter, his eyes baggy and his face pasty from hours of wakefulness, glowered at everyone—except the detective and uniformed officer from New York's police force.

George and Bess sat on easy chairs in one corner. Behind George's chair stood Jack Kale, his hand on George's shoulder. On an ottoman in the other corner sat Alison Kale, and next to her, Nancy Drew, who now prepared to tell her story.

"She assaulted me, officer!" shouted Pieter van

Druten to the police detective. "I want to press charges to the full extent of the law!"

"This man poisoned Sarah Amberly, and killed Maximilian, too," said Nancy gravely, rising to her feet and indicating Pieter. "I'm sure of it."

Ritter looked at the police detective and got a nod to continue before he walked over to Nancy. "Go ahead, let's hear how you came to this so-called conclusion of yours."

Nancy took a long, deep breath. Convincing Joe Ritter was going to be even harder than netting Pieter van Druten had been.

"I felt he was threatening from the first," she began, pacing the room to clear her head. "The way he snapped at Maximilian, the way he tried to control Sarah . . . When she died, I suspected Pieter immediately.

"The problem was, it seemed as though he couldn't have done it. I mean, Bess and George and I saw him at Trump Tower, right about the time the murder was committed—"

"Unbelievable!" gasped Pieter, his pale eyes flashing with hatred. "You saw me there yourself, and yet you have the absolute gall to accuse me—"

"Hold on, buddy. Why don't you let her finish, and then you can yell your head off, okay?" snapped Ritter, his patience thin. He seemed to feel it should have been *him* explaining things, not Nancy, and he wasn't at all comfortable with his position as a part of the audience.

"So," continued Nancy, "at first I didn't think he could have done it. That left two possibilities —Jack Kale and Alison Kale.

"Both of them had reasons for killing Sarah Amberly. She had threatened to disinherit Jack, and she'd quarreled with Alison just the night before. No offense, but both of them are, well—a little unstable, and both of them had plenty of opportunity to give her the overdose.

"Every piece of evidence pointed to one or the other of them—the stolen ruby ring and jewelry box, and the note of Alison's that I found, the one that said 'Kill—Kill—Kill—'"

"Wait a minute!" Ritter jumped to his feet. "You never told me anything about that. I ought to turn you in for obstructing justice!"

"If you'll just wait a few minutes," said Nancy calmly, "I think you'll change your mind about that."

Scowling more than ever, Ritter took his seat again.

"Anyway, as I was saying," Nancy resumed, "all the evidence pointed toward the Kales, and away from van Druten. But I just didn't feel right about it somehow. Sarah herself had told me, whatever happened, not to blame Alison. And everything I found out about Alison after that made me agree with Sarah." Nancy glanced over at Alison, who looked up at her, her grateful face red with embarrassment.

"Alison never liked Pieter van Druten," Nancy went on. "Neither did Jack Kale. In fact, I myself wondered about that. Why would someone as sharp about people as Sarah Amberly give her heart to a man like Pieter? And I realized—she wouldn't."

"You're lying!" growled van Druten. "Sarah and I loved each other! We were completely devoted! This girl is slandering me. Are you going to allow her to malign the dead like this?"

"Let her finish," Ritter barked, pointing at Pieter.

Nancy began pacing the room again. As she went, the eyes of Pieter van Druten followed her every move. Even now, that look of his made her skin crawl.

"My first real clue, if you can call it that, was Sarah's last words. She said: 'The Devil, the Fool, and Death.' I wondered what she meant, until Madame Rosa told me. The Devil, the Fool, and Death are all tarot cards, and according to Madame Rosa they might have stood for people in Sarah's life. Sarah told me, for instance, that I was the Three of Cups. So it stood to reason that she would connect her family with tarot cards, too.

"But which card stood for which person? I remembered the arguments I overheard between

Sarah and the Kales. She'd called Alison a fool, and she told Jack he was a devil—that left only Pieter as the Death card."

Van Druten stood up, his face purple with rage. "If that's the sort of evidence you have against me, I hope you've got yourself a good lawyer, because you're going to need one!"

"I do," said Nancy, looking at her father, who stood by the door now, a package in his hands. "But I don't think I'll need him. Not if you'll hear me out."

She looked over at Ritter, who nodded for her to continue.

"I knew it was only a hunch, but what if Sarah had been trying to tell me who had killed her? I thought about it for hours—and then it came to me.

"The first time I ever saw Sarah, she was shouting at everyone about how her pills were always running low. The night I had to give her a pill to save her life, I counted the pills left in the bottle. There were ten. The next night, after her death, I counted again—there were only seven. The dose indicated on the bottle was one pill every evening. That meant at least two were missing!

"Then it came to me. What if Pieter had put a couple of crushed-up pills in Sarah's tea—she always had a cup in the evening. Then, when she took her normal dose an hour later, an overdose would have resulted, causing death. Pieter only had to make sure he was seen elsewhere at the time of death, and his alibi was ironclad!"

Bess gasped out loud, sitting up on the couch. "You mean when we saw him that night, he had just come from—oh no!" Her hand flew to her mouth in horror.

Nancy ignored Bess's remark. "I felt sure that I was right," she went on. "But if I was, Pieter had committed the perfect crime. Or had he? When we saw him, he was holding an airline ticket.

"Just in case? I wondered. A careful criminal always has a getaway planned. And whoever killed Sarah Amberly was very careful—which is why I never thought Jack Kale killed her, by the way. He's so reckless as a gambler, it wouldn't be like him to plan things out so carefully."

Jack smiled at her from across the room. "You tell 'em, Nancy," he said.

"Well," Nancy resumed, taking a deep breath. "After he bought the ticket, Pieter stopped at the dry cleaners to drop off a shirt. And I thought, why did he do that? One shirt, at ten o'clock at night?

"I managed to get the shirt before it was cleaned. And my dad had it analyzed by Interpol's lab. Dad?"

Carson cleared his throat and pulled the soiled shirt out of the bag. "We just got the results of the test an hour ago. Tea stains," he said, pointing to them. "And traces of Sarah Amberly's medicine —oxytomicin."

"My first hard evidence." Nancy smiled. Pieter van Druten looked as if he were about to explode. On either side of him, two policemen kept watch, just in case he decided to move.

"What about Maximilian?" Ritter wanted to know. "I had him pegged for the killer, to tell you the truth." For the first time, Ritter was speaking to Nancy with some real respect.

"Well, his hatred of the Amberlys was intense. It was almost an obsession. And that made me suspect him," Nancy agreed. "I have a feeling that if I had dug into his background a little, I would have found some old skeletons in the closet, something connected with Sarah and Joshua Amberly. But that's a whole other story.

"When I was pushed," Nancy continued, "down in the basement, I thought he had done it. But when he was killed too, I realized that his game wasn't murder—it was blackmail. And that it must have been the person he was following—Pieter van Druten—who had tried to kill me. Maximilian must have gone down there expecting a payoff. Only he got a payoff he wasn't expecting.

"I checked with the staff," said Nancy. "The night Sarah died, Maximilian was the one who brought her tea from room service. My guess is that he saw Pieter putting the medicine in the tea.

And by the way, Pieter, you slipped up when you left the door of the suite wide open. After Sarah's death, Maximilian must have put two and two together, and put the screws on Pieter. He even warned me not to mess around in matters that didn't concern me. I guess he was trying to protect his little blackmail racket. Unfortunately for him, he messed around with the wrong person."

There was silence in the room. Ritter scratched his head, going over everything Nancy had said.

"Wait—I still don't get it," he said. "Why in the world would van Druten here want to bump off the old lady? All he had to do was marry her, and he would have had everything. Why kill her?"

Nancy looked over at Pieter. He was smiling at her, daring her to explain that one. It was a smile of triumph, a smile that said, "Now I've got you."

"That had me stumped, too." Nancy nodded. "Pieter stood to lose if Sarah died before she married him. I didn't know what to think, until I remembered Alison saying something about Sarah being a 'one-man woman.'

"I thought of all the things Sarah had told me about her dead husband Joshua, about the way she kept his ring on her night table, and I thought, what if Sarah had told Pieter she would *never* marry him?

"And something else—Pieter van Druten was

supposed to have diamond mines in South Africa, so why didn't he know the jewels in the missing jewelry box were fakes? I remember him saying they were very valuable when they were first missing. Either he didn't know their value, or he was trying to make Alison look guilty. Either way, something was fishy. So I had my father check on him through Interpol."

Carson reached into his pocket and handed Nancy an envelope.

"It seems Pieter van Druten was not a diamond mine owner at all, but a well-known con man, who served time in Robbin Island Prison for grand larceny and fraud. And another thing, Pieter van Druten was an alias. This man's real name is Patrick Kale!"

An electric charge ran through the room. Suddenly Pieter shot to his feet, ready to lunge at Nancy. He was restrained just in time by the two burly officers and forced to take his seat again.

"Yes, a distant relative." Nancy nodded. "A con man whose hand is played out in his native country. One day he reads an obituary in the papers—the death of the famous Joshua Amberly, Boston millionaire. Widow Sarah, née Kale—and a plan forms in his mind.

"He's a handsome man, Patrick Kale, suave and debonair. The ladies have always liked him. So he goes to America under another name and gets to know the wealthy widow.

"Sarah Amberly is lonely and likes his company. He's doing well, getting closer to his goal. And then one day, she tells him she can never marry him, that she will always be a 'one-man woman.' And that's when he decides to kill her.

"If he can make it look as if the sister and nephew are behind it, he can then declare his real identity and collect the inheritance. That's why he tried to make Alison look guilty by planting the jewels in her drawer. He overheard Alison begging me to hide them for her, and when she ran off, he stuck a knife through a note she'd written, just to make her look even more suspicious."

Nancy sat down. "So there you have it, Detective Ritter. I'm sorry I didn't share all my information with you in the beginning, but you must remember, you didn't exactly trust me."

"No, I didn't," admitted Ritter. "My apologies, Miss Drew." He went over to Pieter, the soiled shirt in his hands. "This ought to do it for you, Mr. van Druten—or should I say, Mr. Kale?"

Pieter glared at Nancy. "It was a good plan, a perfect plan," he growled. "And it would have worked, too."

"Yes, you're right." Carson nodded. "It would have worked, if your neighbor at the Plaza had been anyone else but Nancy Drew!"

Chapter

Seventeen

WHAT A FANTASTIC show! I'll never forget the music—and those costumes!" Nancy stepped out of the yellow taxi cab as Carson held out his hand to help her. "Thanks, Dad."

Nancy beamed. She and her dad had finally gotten their day together in New York City, and they were both feeling on top of the world.

"It was fun, all right," Carson agreed. "Good old Broadway, where everyone just bursts into song at the drop of a hat," he mused, a little wistfully, Nancy thought. "Wasn't it terrific the way they did that tap number?"

"And when she did that number with the

shadows behind her— Oh, what a show!" Nancy was still sailing. Maybe the next time she and Ned came to New York she could take him to the show too. It would be great to see it again.

"Nancy! Mr. Drew! Wait up!"

Turning around at the top of the Plaza steps, Nancy and Carson saw Bess and George flying toward them.

"Hi, you guys!" Nancy called out in surprise.

"Fancy meeting you here!" said Bess as she and George climbed up to Nancy and her father.

"Coming to see us?" asked Nancy.

"Actually," answered George, "we've been invited to a little party on your floor. Jack Kale is having a few friends by."

"You're invited, too. He told us. Both of you," Bess added, walking through the polished brass and glass door that the doorman held open for them with a smile.

"I'm afraid I have to make some calls before we leave," Carson explained. "You'll have to go without me."

"Well, I'm all packed, so why not?" said Nancy, pressing the elevator button.

"Jack said he may come out and visit River Heights this fall!" Nancy could see the stars in George's eyes.

"Well, that's terrific," said Nancy. "A party sounds great! And here we are." The elevator door opened on the top floor of the grand old hotel.

"Have a good time, girls," Carson replied. "Don't forget, Nancy, we leave in an hour."

"No problem, Dad." The girls waved goodbye to Carson at his door and walked to the Amberly suite.

"I hope there'll be some cute guys here. Maybe Jack has a couple of friends—" Bess fluttered her lashes and grinned.

"Bess, you have a one-track mind." Nancy laughed.

"He's just so adorable, you know?" George seemed to be talking out loud to herself as she knocked on the door of the Amberly suite.

Bess and Nancy shot each other a look and laughed. "You think *I* have a one-track mind?" said Bess. "George seems to be operating on a single orbit herself these days—around Jack Kale."

And there he was at the door. "Hello! Let the party begin!" he said as he opened the door with a flourish. "Come in, ladies."

Sitting on the divan was Alison Kale. For the first time since Nancy had seen her, she actually looked relaxed. Not only that, she was wearing lipstick and an attractive dress that made her look almost pretty.

"Hello, Nancy," she said warmly. "Hello, girls."

"What's the party for, Jack?" asked Nancy, a twinkle in her eye.

Jack raised his eyebrows and smiled. "Isn't it clear as crystal? This is a celebration, my friends. We're inaugurating the long prison career of my dear long-lost fifth cousin, Pieter van Druten."

While Jack ran to get the girls some soda, they glanced around the suite. For the first time, it was filled with people, and there was actually a festive atmosphere about the place. Knots of well-dressed, handsome guys and great-looking girls mingled in cheerful groups all over the huge room.

"Jack has a lot of friends," whispered George in Nancy's ear. "And they're all so *interesting,* too. He introduced me to some of them the other night."

Nancy smiled. This was the way a suite at the Plaza was meant to feel, not creepy and ominous, the way it had been when she'd first seen it.

"And here we are, ladies," Jack announced, handing them their glasses. "To the future!" he said.

"And what does the future hold for Jack Kale?" Nancy asked.

"Nothing like the past, I can promise you that," Jack said. "I'm the Devil no more—scout's honor. I'm not going to steal, or even gamble, ever again. Now I have all the money I need." His expression grew serious. "Thanks to you, Aunt Sarah," he added, raising his glass to the ceiling.

"And, yes, I'm going straight," he added, his exuberant spirits returning. "I'll have you know I even retrieved this little trinket from the pawnshop." He drew the ruby ring from his jacket pocket.

Looking at it, Bess nearly dropped. "Wow!" she cried. "Nancy, it's everything you said it was. I can't believe the size of that rock!"

Cupping it in his palm, Jack walked over to his aunt and held it out to her. "Here, Aunt Alison," he told her. "I know Sarah would want you to have it."

Nancy stole a rapid glance at George. Her eyelids were lowered, and she was staring at Jack with moonbeams in her eyes. "Uh, George," warned Nancy, "better take it easy. The guy may not be a murderer, but he's definitely not for you."

"Oh, no?" asked George, turning to her. "And why not?"

"Just check it out," replied Nancy, pursing her lips. As they spoke, Jack wandered over to one of the other young women and started flirting with her. In seconds, he had an arm around her and was gazing romantically into her eyes.

"See what I mean?" said Nancy.

George looked crestfallen. She heaved a deep sigh and put down her glass. "Oh well"—

she sighed wistfully—"he was nice while he lasted."

Bess and Nancy burst out laughing. "Poor George!" cried Bess. "Don't worry—money, looks, and charm aren't everything!"

"That's right," echoed Nancy, throwing her arm around her disappointed friend. "Of course, they don't hurt, either—"

George couldn't help cracking a smile.

"There's the George Fayne we know and love," cried Nancy happily. "And don't worry—next time I set you up with a suave, handsome millionaire, I'll make sure his blue blood is *true* blue!"

Nancy's next case:

Nancy, Bess, and George fly to Los Angeles to investigate how and why a priceless miniature portrait of Napoleon suddenly burst into flames while being held in a hotel vault. As other Napoleonic relics disappear, it becomes clear that an extortionist is at work. If the owners don't pay up, their priceless treasures will go up in smoke.

Nancy finds herself in a world of luxury and scandal, confronted by offbeat California types, art dealers, socialites, handsome playboys—even a sheik. The Empress's Flame, the gown Josephine wore to Napoleon's coronation, has been targeted by the extortionist. When George tries it on, it bursts into flames! Can Nancy save the priceless gown and her friend's life? Find out in *PLAYING WITH FIRE*, Case #26 in The Nancy Drew Files™.

Forthcoming Titles in the
Nancy Drew Files™ Series

No. 27 Most Likely to Die
No. 28 The Black Widow
No. 29 Pure Poison
No. 30 Death by Design
No. 31 Trouble in Tahiti
No. 32 High Marks For Malice
No. 33 Danger in Disguise
No. 34 Vanishing Act

Gung-ho missions and tense, rollicking investigations – **The Hardy Boys** ™ are unstoppable! And now Simon & Schuster Ltd. are publishing two thrilling titles every month.

The Hardy Boys ™ are back! Frank and Joe don't court danger, it just happens along. As private investigators they ricochet from case to case, investigating, troubleshooting and putting gross wrongs to right. These two young detectives dance with death and untangle dangerous schemes in a series of hard-paced, fast-moving, action-packed adventures.

Books in The Hardy Boys ™ Casefiles Series

No. 11 BROTHER AGAINST BROTHER
No. 12 PERFECT GETAWAY
No. 13 THE BORGIA DAGGER
No. 14 TOO MANY TRAITORS
No. 15 BLOOD RELATIONS
No. 16 LINE OF FIRE

Simon & Schuster publish a wide range of titles from pre-school books to books for adults.

For up-to-date catalogues, please contact:

International Book Distributors
Campus 400
Maylands Avenue
Hemel Hempstead
Herts
HP2 7EZ

Tel. 0442 882255